BOTCHAN

(Master Darling)

By

(The Late Mr.) Kin-nosuke Natsume,

known as

Natsume Sōseki

Professor of English Literature
Imperial University;
Associate Editor of the Tokyo Asahi

TRANSLATED

By

Yasotaro Morri

On the Editorial Staff of
The Kokusai News Agency

Zea Books
Lincoln, Nebraska
2022

This English translation of 坊っちゃん (1906) was
originally published in Tokyo by Ogawa Seibundo in 1918.

ISBN 978-1-60962-221-3 paperback
ISBN 978-1-60962-222-0 ebook
doi: 10.32873/unl.dc.zea.1311

Zea Books are published by the
University of Nebraska-Lincoln Libraries.

Electronic (pdf) edition available online at
https://digitalcommons.unl.edu/zeabook/

Print edition available from Lulu.com at
http://www.lulu.com/spotlight/unllib

University of Nebraska-Lincoln does not discriminate
based upon any protected status. Please go to
http://www.unl.edu/equity/notice-nondiscrimination

A NOTE BY THE TRANSLATOR

NO translation can expect to equal, much less to excel, the original. The excellence of a translation can only be judged by noting how far it has succeeded in reproducing the original tone, colors, style, the delicacy of sentiment, the force of inert strength, the peculiar expressions native to the language with which the original is written, or whatever is its marked characteristic. The ablest can do no more, and to want more than this will be demanding something impossible. Strictly speaking, the only way one can derive full benefit or enjoyment from a foreign work is to read the original, for any intelligence at second-hand never gives the kind of satisfaction which is possible only through the direct touch with the original. Even in the best translated work is probably wanted the subtle vitality natural to the original language, for it defies an attempt, however elaborate, to transmit all there is in the original. Correctness of diction may be there, but spontaneity is gone; it cannot be helped.

The task of the translator becomes doubly hazardous in case of translating a European language into Japanese, or vice versa. Between any of the European languages and Japanese there is no visible kinship in word-form, significance, grammatical system, rhetorical arrangements. It may be said that the inspiration of the two languages is totally different. A want of similarity of customs, habits, traditions, national sentiments and traits makes the work of translation all the more difficult. A novel written in Japanese which had attained national popularity might, when rendered into English, lose its captivating vividness, alluring interest and lasting appeal to the reader.

These remarks are made not in way of excuse for any faulty dictions that may be found in the following pages. Neither are they made out of personal modesty nor of a desire to add undue weight to the present work. They are made in the hope that whoever is good enough to go through the present translation will remember, before he may venture to make criticisms, the kind and extent of difficulties besetting him in his attempts so as not to judge the merit of the original by this translation. Nothing would afford the translator a greater pain than any unfavorable comment on the original based upon this translation. If there be any deserving merits in the following pages the credit is due to the original. Any fault found in its interpretation or in the English version, the whole responsibility is on the translator.

For the benefit of those who may not know the original, it must be stated that "Botchan" by the late Mr. K. Natsume was an epoch-making piece of work. On its first appearance, Mr. Natsume's place and name as the foremost in the new literary school were firmly established. He had written many other novels of more serious intent, of heavier thoughts and of more enduring merits, but it was this "Botchan" that secured him the lasting fame. Its quaint style, dash and vigor in its narration appealed to the public who had become somewhat tired of the stereotyped sort of manner with which all stories had come to be handled.

In its simplest understanding, "Botchan" may be taken as an episode in the life of a son born in Tokyo, hot-blooded, simple-hearted, pure as crystal and sturdy as a towering rock, honest and straight to a fault, intolerant of the least injustice and a volunteer ever ready to champion what he considers right and good. Children may read it as a "story of man who tried to be honest." It is a light, amusing and, at the same time, instructive story, with no tangle of love affairs, no scheme of blood-curdling scenes or nothing startling or sensational in the plot or characters. The story, however, may be regarded as a biting sarcasm on a hypocritical society in which a gang of instructors of dark character at a middle school in a backwoods town plays a prominent part. The hero of the story is made a victim of their annoying intrigues, but finally comes out triumphant by smashing the petty red tape-ism, knocking down the sham pretentions and by actual use of the fist on the Head Instructor and his henchman.

The story will be found equally entertaining as a means of studying the peculiar traits of the native of Tokyo which are characterised by their quick temper, dashing spirit, generosity and by their readiness to resist even the lordly personage if convinced of their own justness, or to kneel down even to a child if they acknowledge their own wrong. Incidentally the touching devotion of the old maid servant Kiyo to the hero will prove a standing reproach to the inconstant, unfaithful servants of which the number is ever increasing these days in Tokyo. The story becomes doubly interesting by the fact that Mr. K. Natsume, when quite young, held a position of teacher of English at a middle school somewhere about the same part of the country described in the story, while he himself was born and brought up in Tokyo.

It may be added that the original is written in an autobiographical style. It is profusely interladed with spicy, catchy colloquials patent to the people of Tokyo for the equals of which we may look to the rattling speeches of notorious Chuck Conners of the Bowery of New York. It should be frankly stated that much difficulty was experienced in getting the corresponding terms in English for those catchy expressions. Strictly speaking, some of them have no English equivalents. Care has been exercised to select what has been thought most appropriate in the judgment of the translator in converting those expressions into English but some of them might provoke disapproval from those of the "cultured" class with "refined" ears. The slangs in English in this translation were taken from an American magazine of world-wide reputation editor of which was not afraid to print of "damn" when necessary, by scorning the timid, conventional way of putting it as "d--n." If the propriety of printing such short ugly words be questioned, the translator is sorry to say that no means now exists of directly bringing him to account for he met untimely death on board the Lusitania when it was sunk by the German submarine.

Thanks are due to Mr. J. R. Kennedy, General Manager, and Mr. Henry Satoh, Editor-in-Chief, both of the Kokusai Tsushin-sha (the International News Agency) of Tokyo and a host of personal friends of the translator whose untiring assistance and kind suggestions have made the present translation possible. Without their sympathetic interests, this translation may not have seen the daylight.

Y. M.
Tokyo, September, 1918.

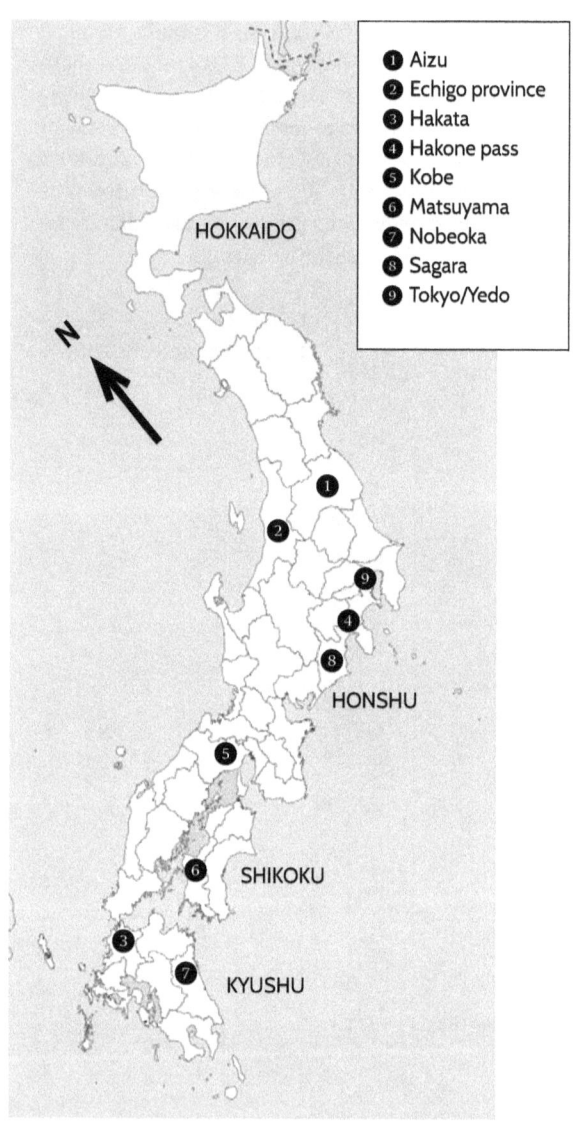

1	Aizu
2	Echigo province
3	Hakata
4	Hakone pass
5	Kobe
6	Matsuyama
7	Nobeoka
8	Sagara
9	Tokyo/Yedo

HOKKAIDO

N

HONSHU

SHIKOKU

KYUSHU

BOTCHAN

(Master Darling)

CHAPTER I.

BECAUSE of an hereditary recklessness, I have been playing always a losing game since my childhood. During my grammar school days, I was once laid up for about a week by jumping from the second story of the school building. Some may ask why I committed such a rash act. There was no particular reason for doing such a thing except I happened to be looking out into the yard from the second floor of the newly-built school house, when one of my classmates, joking, shouted at me; "Say, you big bluff, I'll bet you can't jump down from there! O, you chicken-heart, ha, ha!" So I jumped down. The janitor of the school had to carry me home on his back, and when my father saw me, he yelled derisively, "What a fellow you are to go and get your bones dislocated by jumping only from a second story!"

"I'll see I don't get dislocated next time," I answered.

One of my relatives once presented me with a pen-knife. I was showing it to my friends, reflecting its pretty blades against the rays of the sun, when one of them chimed in that the blades gleamed all right, but seemed rather dull for cutting with.

"Rather dull? See if they don't cut!" I retorted.

"Cut your finger, then," he challenged. And with

"Finger nothing! Here goes!" I cut my thumb slant-wise. Fortunately the knife was small and the bone of the thumb hard enough, so the thumb is still there, but the scar will be there until my death.

About twenty steps to the east edge of our garden, there was a moderate-sized vegetable yard, rising toward the south, and in the centre of which stood a chestnut tree which was dearer to me than life. In the season when the chestnuts were ripe, I used to slip out of the house from the back door early in the morning to pick up the chestnuts which had fallen during the night, and eat them at the school. On the west side of the vegetable yard was the adjoining garden of a pawn shop called Yamashiro-Ya. This shopkeeper's son was a boy about 13 or 14 years old named Kantaro. Kantaro was, it happens, a mollycoddle. Nevertheless he had the temerity to come over the fence to our yard and steal my chestnuts.

One certain evening I hid myself behind a folding-gate of the fence and caught him in the act. Having his retreat cut off he grappled with me in desperation. He was about two years older than, I and, though weak-kneed, was physically the stronger. While I walloped him, he pushed his head against my breast and by chance it slipped inside my sleeve. As this hindered the free action of my arm, I tried to shake him loose, though, his head dangled the further inside, and being no longer able to stand the stifling combat, he bit my bare arm. It was painful. I held him fast against the fence, and by a dexterous foot twist sent him down flat on his back. Kantaro broke the fence and as the ground belonging to Yamashiro-ya was about six feet lower than the vegetable yard, he fell headlong to his own territory with a thud. As he rolled off he tore away the sleeve in which his head had been enwrapped, and my arm recovered a sudden freedom of movement. That night when my mother went to Yamashiro-Ya to apologize, she brought back that sleeve.

Besides the above, I did many other mischiefs. With Kaneko of a carpenter shop and Kaku of a fish-market, I once ruined a carrot patch of one Mosaku. The sprouts were just shooting out and the patch was covered with straws to ensure their even healthy growth. Upon this straw-covered patch we three wrestled for fully half a day, and consequently thoroughly smashed all the sprouts. Also I once filled up a well which watered some rice fields owned by one Furukawa, and he followed me with kicks. The well was so devised that from a large bamboo pole, sunk deep into the ground, the water issued and irrigated the rice fields. Ignorant of the mechanical side of this irrigating method at that time, I stuffed the bamboo pole with stones and sticks, and satisfied that no more water came up, I returned home and was eating supper when Furukawa, fiery red with anger, burst into our house with howling protests. I believe the affair was settled on our paying for the damage.

Father did not like me in the least, and mother always sided with my big brother. This brother's face was pale-ish white, and he had a fondness for taking the part of an actress at the theatre.

"This fellow will never amount to much," father used to remark when he saw me.

"He's so reckless that I worry about his future," I often heard mother say of me. Exactly; I have never amounted to much. I am just as you see me; no wonder my future used to cause anxiety to my mother. I am living without becoming but a jailbird.

Two or three days previous to my mother's death, I took it into my head to turn a somersault in the kitchen, and painfully hit my ribs against the corner of the stove. Mother was very angry at this and told me not to show my face again, so I went to a relative to stay with. While there, I received the news that my mother's illness had become very serious, and that after all efforts for her recovery, she was dead. I came home thinking that I should have behaved better if I had known the conditions were so serious as that. Then that big brother of mine denounced me as wanting in filial piety, and that I had caused her untimely death. Mortified at this, I slapped his face, and thereupon received a sound scolding from father.

After the death of mother, I lived with father and brother. Father did nothing, and always said "You're no good" to my face. What he meant by "no good" I am yet to understand. A funny dad he was. My brother was to be seen studying English hard, saying that he was going to be a businessman. He was like a girl by nature, and so "sassy" that we two were never on good terms, and had to fight it out about once every ten days. When we played a chess game one day, he placed a chessman as a "waiter," — a cowardly tactic this, — and had hearty laugh on me by seeing me in a fix. His manner was so trying that time that I banged a chessman on his forehead which was injured a little bit and bled. He told all about this to father, who said he would disinherit me.

Then I gave up myself for lost, and expected to be really disinherited. But our maid Kiyo, who had been with us for ten years or so, interceded on my behalf, and tearfully apologized for me, and by her appeal my father's wrath was softened. I did not regard him, however, as one to be afraid of in any way, but rather felt sorry for our Kiyo. I had heard that Kiyo was of a decent, well-to-do family, but being driven to poverty at the time of the Restoration, had to work as a servant. So she was an old woman by this time. This old woman, — by what affinity, as the Buddhists say, I don 't know, — loved me a great deal. Strange, indeed! She was almost blindly fond of me, — me, whom mother became thoroughly disgusted with three days before her death; whom father considered a most aggravating proposition all the year round, and whom the neighbors cordially hated as the local bully among the youngsters. I had long reconciled myself to the fact that my nature was far from being attractive to others, and so didn't mind if I were treated as a piece of wood; so I thought it uncommon that Kiyo should pet me like that. Sometimes in the kitchen, when there was nobody around, she would praise me saying that I was straightforward and of a good disposition. What she meant by that exactly, was not clear to me, however. If I were of so good a nature as she said, I imagined those other than Kiyo should accord me a better treatment. So whenever Kiyo said to me anything of the kind, I used to answer that I did not like passing compliments. Then she would remark; "That's the very reason I say you are of a good disposition," and would gaze at me with absorbing tenderness. She seemed to recreate me by her own imagination, and was proud of the fact. I felt even chilled through my marrow at her constant attention to me.

After my mother was dead, Kiyo loved me still more. In my simple reasoning, I wondered why she had taken such a fancy to me. Sometimes I thought it quite futile on her part, that she had better quit that sort of thing, which was bad for her. But she loved me just the same. Once in a while she would buy, out of her own pocket, some cakes or sweet-meats for me. When the night was cold, she would secretly buy some noodle powder, and bring all unawares hot noodle gruel to my bed; or sometimes she would even buy a bowl of steaming noodles from the peddler. Not only with edibles, but she was generous alike with socks, pencils, note books, etc. And she even furnished me, — this happened some time later, — with about three yen. I did not ask her for the money; she offered it from her own good will by bringing it to my room, saying that I might be in need of some cash. This, of course, embarrassed me, but as she was so insistent I consented to borrow it. I confess I was really glad of the money. I put it in a bag, and carried it in my pocket. While about the house, I happened to drop the bag into a cesspool. Helpless, I told Kiyo how I had lost the money, and at once she fetched a bamboo stick, and said she will get it for me. After a while I heard a splashing sound of water about our family well, and going there, saw Kiyo washing the bag strung on the end of the stick. I opened the bag and found the color of the three one-yen bills turned to faint yellow and designs fading. Kiyo dried them at an open fire and handed them over to me, asking if they were all right. I smelled them and said; "They stink yet."

"Give them to me I'll get them changed." She took those three bills, and, — I do not know how she went about it, — brought three yen in silver. I forget now upon what I spent the three yen. "I'll pay you back soon," I said at the time, but didn't. I could not now pay it back even if I wished to do so with ten times the amount.

When Kiyo gave me anything she did so always when both father and brother were out. Many things I do not like, but what I most detest is the monopolizing of favors behind some one else's back. Bad as my relations were with my brother, still I did not feel justified in accepting candies or color-pencils from Kiyo without my brother's knowledge. "Why do you give those things only to me and not to my brother also?" I asked her once, and she answered quite unconcernedly that my brother may be left to himself as his father bought him everything. That was partiality; father was obstinate, but I am sure he was not a man who would indulge in favoritism. To Kiyo, however, he might have looked that way. There is no doubt that Kiyo was blind to the extent of her undue indulgence with me. She was said to have come from a well-to-do family, but the poor soul was uneducated, and it could not be helped. All the same, you cannot tell how prejudice will drive one to the extremes. Kiyo seemed quite sure that some day I would achieve high position in society and become famous. Equally she was sure that my brother, who was spending his hours studiously, was only good for his white skin, and would stand no show in the future. Nothing can beat an old woman for this sort of thing, I tell you. She firmly believed that whoever she liked would become famous, while whoever she hated would not. I did not have at that time any particular object in my life. But the persistency with which Kiyo declared that I would be a great man some day, made me speculate myself that after all I might become one. How absurd it seems to me now when I recall those days. I asked her once what kind of a man I should be, but she seemed to have formed no concrete idea as to that; only she said that I was sure to live in a house with grand entrance hall, and ride in a private rikisha.

And Kiyo seemed to have decided for herself to live with me when I became independent and occupy my own house. "Please let me live with you," — she repeatedly asked of me. Feeling somewhat that I should eventually be able to own a house, I answered her "Yes," as far as such an answer went. This woman, by the way, was strongly imaginative. She questioned me what place I liked, Kojimachi-ku or Azabu-ku? — and suggested that I should have a swing in our garden, that one room be enough for European style, etc., planning everything to suit her own fancy. I did not then care a straw for anything like a house; so neither Japanese nor European style was much of use to me, and I told her to that effect. Then she would praise me as uncovetous and clean of heart. Whatever I said, she had praise for me.

I lived, after the death of mother, in this fashion for five or six years. I had kicks from father, had rows with brother, and had candies and praise from Kiyo. I cared for nothing more; I thought this was enough. I imagined all other boys were leading about the same kind of life. As Kiyo frequently told me, however, that I was to be pitied, and was unfortunate, I imagined that that might be so. There was nothing that particularly worried me except that father was too tight with my pocket money, and this was rather hard on me.

In January of the 6th year after mother's death, father died of apoplexy. In April of the same year, I graduated from a middle school, and two months later, my brother graduated from a business college. Soon he obtained a job in the Kyushu branch of a certain firm and had to go there, while I had to remain in Tokyo and continue my study. He proposed the sale of our house and the realization of our property, to which I answered "Just as you like it." I had no intention of depending upon him anyway. Even were he to look after me, I was sure of his starting some thing which would eventually end in a smash-up as we were prone to quarrel on the least pretext. It was because in order to receive his protection that I should have to bow before such a fellow, that I resolved that I would live by myself even if I had to do milk delivery. Shortly afterwards he sent for a second-hand dealer and sold for a song all the bric-a-brac which had been handed down from ages ago in our family. Our house and lot were sold, through the efforts of a middleman to a wealthy person. This transaction seemed to have netted a goodly sum to him, but I know nothing as to the detail.

For one month previous to this, I had been rooming in a boarding house in Kanda-ku, pending a decision as to my future course. Kiyo was greatly grieved to see the house in which she had lived so many years change ownership, but she was helpless in the matter,

"If you were a little older, you might have inherited this house," she once remarked in earnest.

If I could have inherited the house through being a little older, I ought to have been able to inherit the house right then. She knew nothing, and believed the lack of age only prevented my coming into the possession of the house.

Thus I parted from my brother, but the disposal of Kiyo was a difficult proposition. My brother was, of course, unable to take her along, nor was there any danger of her following him so far away as Kyushu, while I was in a small room of a boarding house, and might have to clear out anytime at that. There was no way out, so I asked her if she intended to work somewhere else. Finally she answered me definitely that she would go to her nephew's and wait until I started my own house and get married. This nephew was a clerk in the Court of Justice, and being fairly well off, had invited Kiyo before more than once to come and live with him, but Kiyo preferred to stay with us, even as a servant, since she had become well used to our family. But now I think she thought it better to go over to her nephew than to start a new life as servant in a strange house. Be that as it may, she advised me to have my own household soon, or get married, so she would come and help me in housekeeping. I believe she liked me more than she did her own kin.

My brother came to me, two days previous to his departure for Kyushu, and giving me 600 yen, said that I might begin a business with it, or go ahead with my study, or spend it in any way I liked, but that that would be the last he could spare. It was a commendable act for my brother. What! about only 600 yen! I could get along without it, I thought, but as his unusually simple manner appealed to me, I accepted the offer with thanks. Then he produced 50 yen, requesting me to give it to Kiyo next time I saw her, which I readily complied with. Two days after, I saw him off at the Shimbashi Station, and have not set my eyes on him ever since.

Lying in my bed, I meditated on the best way to spend that 600 yen. A business is fraught with too much trouble, and besides it was not my calling. Moreover with only 600 yen no one could open a business worth the name. Were I even able to do it, I was far from being educated, and after all, would lose it. Better let investments alone, but study more with the money. Dividing the 600 yen into three, and by spending 200 yen a year, I could study for three years. If kept at one study with bulldog tenacity for three years, I should be able to learn something. Then the selection of a school was the next problem. By nature, there is no branch of study whatever which appeals to my taste. Nix on languages or literature! The new poetry was all Greek to me; I could not make out one single line of twenty. Since I detested every kind of study, any kind of study should have been the same to me. Thinking thus, I happened to pass front of a school of physics, and seeing a sign posted for the admittance of more students, I thought this might be a kind of "affinity," and having asked for the prospectus, at once filed my application for entrance. When I think of it now, it was a blunder due to my hereditary recklessness.

For three years I studied about as diligently as ordinary fellows, but not being of a particularly brilliant quality, my standing in the class was easier to find by looking up from the bottom. Strange, isn't it, that when three years were over, I graduated? I had to laugh at myself, but there being no reason for complaint, I passed out.

Eight days after my graduation, the principal of the school asked me to come over and see him. I wondered what he wanted, and went. A middle school in Shikoku was in need of a teacher of mathematics for forty yen a month, and he sounded me to see if I would take it. I had studied for three years, but to tell the truth, I had no intention of either teaching or going to the country. Having nothing in sight, however, except teaching, I readily accepted the offer. This too was a blunder due to hereditary recklessness.

I accepted the position, and so must go there. The three years of my school life I had seen confined in a small room, but with no kick coming or having no rough house. It was a comparatively easy going period in my life. But now I had to pack up. Once I went to Kamakura on a picnic with my classmates while I was in the grammar school, and that was the first and last, so far, that I stepped outside of Tokyo since I could remember. This time I must go darn far away, that it beats Kamakura by a mile. The prospective town is situated on the coast, and looked the size of a needle-point on the map. It would not be much to look at anyway. I knew nothing about the place or the people there. It did not worry me or cause any anxiety. I had simply to travel there and that was the annoying part.

Once in a while, since our house was no more, I went to Kiyo's nephew's to see her. Her nephew was unusually good-natured, and whenever I called upon her, he treated me well if he happened to be at home. Kiyo would boost me sky high to her nephew right to my face. She went so far once as to say that when I had graduated from school, I would purchase a house somewhere in Kojimachi-ku and get a position in a government office. She decided everything in her own way, and talked of it aloud, and I was made an unwilling and bashful listener. I do not know how her nephew weighed her tales of self-indulgence on me. Kiyo was a woman of the old type, and seemed, as if it was still the days of Feudal Lords, to regard her nephew equally under obligation to me even as she was herself.

After settling about my new position, I called upon her three days previous to my departure. She was sick abed in a small room, but, on seeing me she got up and immediately inquired;

"Master Darling; when do you begin house keeping?" She evidently thought as soon as a fellow finishes school, money comes to his pocket by itself. But then how absurd to call such a "great man," "Darling." I told her simply that I should let the house proposition go for some time, as I had to go to the country. She looked greatly disappointed, and blankly smoothed her gray-haired side-locks. I felt sorry for her, and said comfortingly; "I am going away, but will come back soon. I'll return in the vacation next summer, sure," Still as she appeared not fully satisfied, I added;

"Will bring you back a surprise. What do you

like?" She wished to eat "sasa-ame"* of Echigo province. I had never heard of "sasa-ame" of Echigo. To begin with, the location is entirely different.

"There seems to be no 'sasa-ame' in the country where I'm going," I explained, and she rejoined; "Then, in what direction?" I answered "westward" and she came back with "Is it on the other side of Hakone?" This give-and take conversation proved too much for me.

On the day of my departure, she came to my room early in the morning and helped me to pack up. She put into my carpet-bag tooth powder, toothbrush and towels which she said she had bought at a dry goods store on her way. I protested that I did not want them, but she was insistent. We rode in rikishas to the station. Coming up the platform, she gazed at me from outside the car, and said in a low voice;

"This may be our last good-by. Take care of yourself."

Her eyes were full of tears. I did not cry, but was almost going to. After the train had run some distance, thinking it would be all right now, I poked my head out of the window and looked back. She was still there. She looked very small.

---

* Sasa-ame is a kind of rice-jelly wrapped with sasa, or the bamboo leaves, well-known as a product of Echigo province.

CHAPTER II.

WITH a long, sonorous whistle the steamer which I was aboard came to a standstill, and a boat was seen making toward us from the shore. The man rowing the boat was stark naked, except for a piece of red cloth girt round his loins. A barbarous place, this! though he may have been excused for it in such hot weather as it was. The sun's rays were strong and the water glimmered in such strange colors as to dazzle one's sight if gazed at it for long. I had been told by a clerk of the ship that I was to get off here. The place looked like a fishing village about the size of Omori. Great Scott! I wouldn't stay in such a hole, I thought, but I had to get out. So, down I jumped first into the boat, and I think five or six others followed me. After loading about four large boxes besides, the red-cloth rowed us ashore. When the boat struck the sand, I was again the first to jump out, and right away I accosted a skinny urchin standing near-by, asking him where the middle school was. The kid answered blankly that he did not know. Confound the dull-head! Not to know where the middle school was, living in such a tiny bit of a town. Then a man wearing a rig with short, queer shaped sleeves approached me and bade me follow. I walked after him and was taken to an inn called Minato-Ya. The maids of the inn, who gave me a disagreeable impression, chorused at sight of me; "Please step inside." This discouraged me in proceeding further, and I asked them, standing at the doorway, to show me the middle school. On being told that the middle school was about four miles away by rail, I became still more discouraged at putting up there. I snatched my two valises from the man with queer-shaped sleeves who had guided me so far, and strode away. The people of the inn looked after me with a dazed expression.

The station was easily found, and a ticket bought without any fuss. The coach I got in was about as dignified as a match-box. The train rambled on for about five minutes, and then I had to get off. No wonder the fare was cheap; it cost only three sen. I then hired a rikisha and arrived at the middle school, but school was already over and nobody was there. The teacher on night-duty was out just for a while, said the janitor, — the night-watch was taking life easy, sure. I thought of visiting the principal, but being tired, ordered the rikishaman to take me to a hotel. He did this with much alacrity and led me to a hotel called Yamashiro-Ya. I felt it rather amusing to find the name Yamashiro-Ya the same as that of Kantaro's house.

They ushered me to a dark room below the stairway. No one could stay in such a hot place! I said I did not like such a warm room, but the maid dumped my valises on the floor and left me, mumbling that all the other rooms were occupied. So I took the room though it took some resolution to stand the weltering heat. After a while, the maid said the bath was ready, and I took one. On my way back from the bath room, I peeped about, and found many rooms, which looked much cooler than mine, vacant. Sunnovgun! They had lied. By'm-by, she fetched my supper. Although the room was hot, the meal was a deal better than the kind I used to have in my boarding house.

While waiting on me, she questioned me where I was from, and I said, "from Tokyo." Their she asked; "Isn't Tokyo a nice place?" and I shot back, "Bet 'tis." About the time the maid had reached the kitchen, loud laughs were heard. There was nothing doing, so I went to bed, but could not sleep. Not only was it hot, But noisy, — about five times noisier than my boarding house. While snoozing, I dreamed of Kiyo. She was eating "sasa-ame" of Echigo province without taking off the wrapper of bamboo leaves. I tried to stop her saying bamboo leaves may do her harm, but she replied, "O, no, these leaves are very helpful for the health," and ate them with much relish. Astounded, I laughed "Ha, ha, ha!" and so awoke. The maid was opening the outside shutters. The weather was just as clear as the previous day.

I had heard once before that when travelling, one should give "tea money" to the hotel or inn where he stops; that unless this "tea money" is given, the hostelry would accord him rather rough treatment. It must have been on account of my being slow in the fork-over of this "tea money" that they had huddled me into such a narrow, dark room. Likewise my shabby clothes and the carpet bags and satin umbrella must have been accountable for it. Took me for a piker, eh? those hayseeds! I would give them a knocker with "tea money." I left Tokyo with about 30 yen in my pocket, which remained from my school expenses. Taking off the railway and steamship fare, and other incidental expenses, I had still about 14 yen in my pocket. I could give them all I had; — what did I care, I was going to get a salary now. All country folk are tight-wads, and one 5-yen bill would hit them square. Now watch and see. Having washed myself, I returned to my room and waited, and the maid of the night before brought in my breakfast. Waiting on me with a tray, she looked at me with a sort of sulphuric smile. Rude! Is any parade marching on my face? I should say. Even my face is far better than that of the maid. I intended of giving "tea money" after breakfast, but I became disgusted, and taking out one 5-yen bill told her to take it to the office later. The face of the maid became then shy and awkward. After the meal, I left for the school. The maid did not have my shoes polished.

I had had vague idea of the direction of the school as I rode to it the previous day, so turning two or three corners, I came to the front gate. From the gate to the entrance the walk was paved with granite. When I had passed to the entrance in the rikisha, this walk made so outlandishly a loud noise that I had felt coy. On my way to the school, I met a number of the students in uniforms of cotton drill and they all entered this gate. Some of them were taller than I and looked much stronger. When I thought of teaching fellows of this ilk, I was impressed with a queer sort of uneasiness. My card was taken to the principal, to whose room I was ushered at once. With scant mustache, dark-skinned and big-eyed, the principal was a man who looked like a badger. He studiously assumed an air of superiority, and saying he would like to see me do my best, handed the note of appointment, stamped big, in a solemn manner. This note I threw away into the sea on my way back to Tokyo. He said he would introduce me to all my fellow teachers, and I was to show to each one of them the note of appointment. What a bother! It would be far better to stick this note up in the teachers' room for three days instead of going through such a monkey process.

The teachers would not be all in the room until the bugle for the first hour was sounded. There was plenty of time. The principal took out his watch, and saying that he would acquaint me particularly with the school by-and-bye, he would only furnish me now with general matters, and started a long lecture on the spirit of education. For a while I listened to him with my mind half away somewhere else, but about half way through his lecture, I began to realize that I should soon be in a bad fix. I could not do, by any means, all he expected of me. He expected that I should make myself an example to the students, should become an object of admiration for the whole school or should exert my moral influence, besides teaching technical knowledge in order to become a real educator, or something ridiculously high-sounding. No man with such admirable qualities would come so far away for only 40 yen a month! Men are generally alike. If one gets excited, one is liable to fight, I thought, but if things are to be kept on in the way the principal says, I could hardly open my mouth to utter anything, nor take a stroll around the place. If they wanted me to fill such an onerous post, they should have told all that before. I hate to tell a lie; I would give it up as having been cheated, and get out of this mess like a man there and then. I had only about 9 yen left in my pocket after tipping the hotel 5 yen. Nine yen would not take me back to Tokyo. I had better not have tipped the hotel; what a pity! However, I would be able to manage it some-how. I considered it better to run short in my return expenses than to tell a lie.

"I cannot do it the way you want me to. I return this appointment."

I shoved back the note. The principal winked his badger-like eyes and gazed at me. Then he said;

"What I have said just now is what I desire of you. I know well that you cannot do all I want. So don't worry."

And he laughed. If he knew it so well already, what on earth did he scare me for?

Meanwhile the bugle sounded, being followed by bustling noises in the direction of the class rooms. All the teachers would be now ready, I was told, and I followed the principal to the teachers' room. In a spacious rectangular room, they sat each before a ta-ble lined along the walls. When I entered the room, they all glanced at me as if by previous agreement. Did they think my face was for a show? Then, as per instructions, I introduced myself and showed the note to each one of them. Most of them left their chairs and made a slight bow of acknowledgement. But some of the more painfully polite took the note and read it and respectfully returned it to me, just like the cheap performances at a rural show! When I came to the fifteenth, who was the teacher of phys-ical training, I became impatient at repeating the same old thing so often. The other side had to do it only once, but my side had to do it fifteen times. They ought to have had some sympathy.

Among those I met in the room there was Mr. Blank who was head teacher. Said he was a Bachelor of Arts. I suppose he was a great man since he was a graduate from Imperial University and had such a title. He talked in a strangely effeminate voice like a woman. But what surprised me most was that he wore a flannel shirt. However thin it might be, flannel is flannel and must have been pretty warm at that time of the year. What painstaking dress is required which will be becoming to a B. A.! And it was a red shirt; wouldn't that kill you! I heard afterwards that he wears a red shirt all the year round. What a strange affliction! According to his own explanation, he has his shirts made to order for the sake of his health as the red color is beneficial to the physical condition. Unnecessary worry, this, for that being the case, he should have had his coat and hakama also in red. And there was one Mr. Koga, teacher of English, whose complexion was very pale. Pale-faced people are usually thin, but this man was pale and fat. When I was attending grammar school, there was one Tami Asai in our class, and his father was just as pale as this Koga. Asai was a farmer, and I asked Kiyo if one's face would become pale if he took up farming. Kiyo said it was not so; Asai ate always Hubbard squash of "uranari"* and that was the reason. Thereafter when I saw any man pale and fat, I took it for granted that it was the result of his having eaten too much of squash of "uranari." This English teacher was surely subsisting upon squash. However, what the meaning of "uranari" is, I do not know. I asked Kiyo once, but she only laughed. Probably she did not know. Among the teachers of mathematics, there was

---

* Means the last crop

one named Hotta. This was a fellow of massive body, with hair closely cropped. He looked like one of the old-time devilish priests who made the Eizan temple famous. I showed him the note politely; but he did not even look at it, and blurted out;

"You're the man newly appointed, eh? Come and see me sometime, ha, ha, ha!"

Devil take his: "Ha, ha, ha!" Who would go to see a fellow so void of the sense of common decency! I gave this priest from this time the nick name of Porcupine.

The Confucian teacher was strict in his manner as becoming to his profession. "Arrived yesterday? You must be tired. Start teaching already? Working hard, indeed!" — and so on. He was an old man, quite sociable and talkative.

The teacher of drawing was altogether like a cheap actor. He wore a thin, flappy haori of sukiya, and, toying with a fan, he giggled; "Where from? eh? Tokyo? Glad to hear that. You make another of our group. I'm a Tokyo kid myself."

If such a fellow prided himself on being a Tokyo kid, I wished I had never been born in Tokyo. I might go on writing about each one of them, for there are many, but I stop here otherwise there will be no end to it.

When my formal introduction was over, the principal said that I might go for the day, but I should make arrangements as to the class hours, etc., with the head teacher of mathematics and begin teaching from the day after the morrow. Asked who was the head teacher of mathematics, I found that he was no other than that Porcupine. Holy smokes! was I to serve under him? I was disappointed. "Say, where are you stopping? Yamashiro-Ya? Well, I'll come and talk it over."

So saying, Porcupine, chalk in hand, left the room to his class. That was rather humiliating for a head-teacher to come over and see his subordinate, but it was better than to call me over to him.

After leaving the school, I thought of returning straight to the hotel, but as there was nothing to do, I decided to take in a little of the town, and started walking about following my nose. I saw prefectural building; it was an old structure of the last century. Also I saw the barracks; they were less imposing than those of the Azabu Regiment, Tokyo. I passed through the main street. The width of the street is about one half that of Kagurazaka, and its aspect is inferior. What about a castle-town of 250,000-koku Lord! Pity the fellows who get swell-headed in such a place as a castle-town!

While I walked about musing like this, I found myself in front of Yamashiro-Ya. The town was much narrower than I had been led to believe.

"I think I have seen nearly all. Guess I'll return and eat." And I entered the gate. The mistress of the hotel who was sitting at the counter, jumped out of her place at my appearance, and with "Are you back, Sire!" scraped the floor with her forehead. When I took my shoes off and stepped inside, the maid took me to an upstairs room that had become vacant. It was a front room of 15 mats (about 90 square feet). I had never before lived in so splendid a room as this. As it was quite uncertain when I should again be able to occupy such a room in future, I took off my European dress, and with only a single Japanese summer coat on, sprawled in the centre of the room in the shape of the Japanese letter "big" (大). I found it very refreshing.

After luncheon I at once wrote a letter to Kiyo. I hate most to write letters because I am poor at sentence-making and also poor in my stock of words. Neither did I have any place to which to address my letters. However, Kiyo might be getting anxious. It would not do to let her worry lest she think the steamer which I boarded had been wrecked and I was drowned, — so I braced up and wrote a long one. The body of the letter was as follows: "Arrived yesterday. A dull place. Am sleeping in a room of 15 mats. Tipped the hotel five yen as tea money. The housewife of the hotel scraped the floor with her forehead. Couldn't sleep last night. Dreamed Kiyo eat sasa-ame together with the bamboo-leaf wrappers. Will return next summer. Went to the school to-day and nicknamed all the fellows. 'Badger' for the principal, 'Red Shirt' for the head-teacher, 'Hubbard Squash' for the teacher of English, 'Porcupine' the teacher of mathematics and 'Clown' for that of drawing. Will write you many other things soon. Good bye."

When I finished writing the letter, I felt better and sleepy. So I slept in the centre of the room, as I had done before, in the letter "big" shape (大). No dream this time, and I had a sound sleep.

"Is this the room?" — a loud voice was heard, — a voice which woke me up, and Porcupine entered.

"How do you do? What you have to do in the school ——" he began talking shop as soon as I got up and rattled me much. On learning my duties in the school, there seemed to be no difficulty, and I decided to accept. If only such were what was expected of me, I would not be surprised were I told to start not only two days hence but even from the following day. The talk on business over, Porcupine said that he did not think it was my intention to stay in such a hotel all the time, that he would find a room for me in a good boarding house, and that I should move.

"They wouldn't take in another from anybody else but I can do it right away. The sooner the better. Go and look at the room to-day, move tomorrow and start teaching from the next day. That'll be all nice and settled."

He seemed satisfied by arranging all by himself. Indeed, I should not be able to occupy such a room for long. I might have to blow in all of my salary for the hotel bill and yet be short of squaring it. It was pity to leave the hotel so soon after I had just shone with a 5-yen tip. However, it being decidedly convenient to move and get settled early if I had to move at all, I asked Porcupine to get that room for me. He told me then to come over with him and see the house at any rate, and I did. The house was situated mid-way up a hill at the end of the town, and was a quiet one. The boss was said to be a dealer in antique curios, called Ikagin, and his wife was about four years his senior. I learned the English word "witch" when I was in the middle school, and this woman looked exactly like one. But as she was another man's wife, what did I care if she was a witch. Finally I decided to live in the house from the next day. On our way back Porcupine treated me to a cup of ice-water. When I first met him in the school, I thought him a disgustingly overbearing fellow, but judging by the way he had looked after me so far, he appeared not so bad after all. Only the seemed, like me, impatient by nature and of quick temper. I heard afterward that he was liked most by all the students in the school.

CHAPTER III

MY teaching began at last. When I entered the class-room and stepped upon the platform for the first time, I felt somewhat strange. While lecturing, I wondered if a fellow like me could keep up the profession of public instructor. The students were noisy. Once in a while, they would holler "Teacher!" "Teacher," — it was "going some." I had been calling others "teacher" every day so far, in the school of physics, but in calling others "teacher" and being called one, there is a wide gap of difference. It made me feel as if some one was tickling my soles. I am not a sneakish fellow, nor a coward; only — it's a pity —I lack audacity. If one calls me "teacher" aloud, it gives me a shock similar to that of hearing the noon-gun in Marunouchi when I was hungry. The first hour passed away in a dashing manner And it passed away without encountering any knotty questions. As I returned to the teachers' room, Porcupine asked me how it was. I simply answered "well," and he seemed satisfied.

When I left the teachers' room, chalk in hand, for the second hour class, I felt as if I was invading the enemy's territory. On entering the room, I found the students for this hour were all big fellows. I am a Tokyo kid, delicately built and small, and did not appear very impressive even in my elevated position. If it comes to a scraping, I can hold my own even with wrestlers, but I had no means of appearing awe-inspiring, merely by the aid of my tongue, to so many as forty such big chaps before me. Believing, however, that it would set a bad precedent to show these country fellows any weakness, I lectured rather loudly and in brusque tone. During the first part the students were taken aback and listened literally with their mouths open. "That's one on you!" I thought. Elated by my success; I kept on lecturing in this tone, when one who looked the strongest, sitting in the middle of the front row, stood up suddenly and called "Teacher!" There it goes! — I thought, and asked him what it was.

"A-ah sa-ay, you talk too quick. A-ah ca-an't you make it a leetle slow? Aah?" "A-ah ca-an't you?" "A-ah?" was altogether dull.

" If I talk too fast, I'll make it slow, but I'm a Tokyo fellow, and can't talk the way you do. If you don't understand it, better wait until you do."

So I answered him. In this way the second hour was closed better than I had expected. Only, as I was about to leave the class, one of the students asked me, "A-ah say, won't you please do them for me?" and showed me some problems in geometry which I was sure I could not solve. This proved to be somewhat a damper on me. But, helpless, I told him I could not make them out, and telling him that I would show him how next time, hastily got out of the room. And all of them raised "Whee—ee!" Some of them were heard saying "He doesn't know much." Don't take a teacher for an encyclopaedia! If I could work out such hard questions as these easily, I would not be in such a backwoods town for forty yen a month. I returned to the teachers' room.

"How was it this time?" asked Porcupine. I said "Umh." But not satisfied with "Um " only, I added that all the students in this school were boneheads. He put up a whimsical face.

The third and the fourth hour and the first hour in the afternoon were more or less the same. In all the classes I attended, I made some kind of blunder. I realised that the profession of teaching was not quite so easy a calling as might have appeared. My teaching for the day was finished but I could not get away. I had to wait alone until three o'clock. I understood that at three o'clock the students of my classes would finish cleaning up the rooms and report to me, whereupon I would go over the rooms. Then I would run through the students' roll, and then be free to go home. Outrageous, indeed, to keep one chained to the school, staring at the empty space when he had nothing more to do, even though he was "bought" by a salary! Other fellow teachers, however, meekly submitted to the regulation, and believing it not well for me, — a new comer — to fuss about it, I stood it. On my way home, I appealed to Porcupine as to the absurdity of keeping me there till three o'clock regardless of my having nothing to do in the school. He said "Yes" and laughed. But he became serious and in an advisory manner told me not to make many complaints about the school.

"Talk to me only, if you want to. There are some queer guys around."

As we parted at the next corner, I did not have time to hear more from him.

On reaching my room, the boss of the house came to me saying, "Let me serve you tea." I expected he was going to treat me to some good tea since he said "Let me serve you," but he simply made himself at home and drank my own tea. Judging by this, I thought he might be practising "Let me serve you" during my absence. The boss said that he was fond of antique drawings and curios and finally had decided to start in that business.

"You look like one quite taken about art. Suppose you begin patronizing my business just for fun as er —connoisseur of art?"

It was the least expected kind of solicitation. Two years ago, I went to the Imperial Hotel (Tokyo) on an errand, and I was taken for a locksmith. When I went to see the Daibutsu at Kamakura, having wrapped up myself from head to toe with a blanket, a rikishaman addressed me as "Gov'ner." I have been mistaken on many occasions for as many things, but none so far has counted on me as a probable connoisseur of art. One should know better by my appearance. Any one who aspires to be a patron of art is usually pictured, — you may see in any drawing, — with either a hood on his head, or carrying a tanzaku* in his hand. The fellow who calls me a connoisseur of art and pretends to mean it, may be surely as crooked as a dog's hind legs. I told him I did not like such artstuff, which is usually favored by retired people. He laughed, and remarking that that nobody liked it at first, but once in it, will find it so fascinating that he will hardly get over it, served tea for himself and drank it in a grotesque manner. I may say that I had asked him the night before to buy some tea for me, but I did not like such a bitter, heavy kind. One swallow seemed to act right on my stomach. I told him to buy a kind not so bitter as that, and he answered "All

---

* A tanzaku is a long, narrow strip of stiff paper on which a Japanese poem is written.

right, Sir," and drank another cup. The fellow seemed never to know of having enough of anything so long as it was another man's. After he left the room, I prepared for the morrow and went to bed.

Everyday thereafter I attended at the school and worked as per regulations. Every day on my return, the boss came to my room with the same old "Let me serve you tea." In about a week I understood the school in a general way, and had my own idea as to the personality of the boss and his wife. I heard from one of my fellow teachers that the first week to one month after the receipt of the appointment worried them most as to whether they had been favorably received among the students. I never felt anything on that score. Blunders in the class room once in a while caused me chagrin, but in about half an hour everything would clear out of my head. I am a fellow who, by nature, can't be worrying long about anything even if I try to. I was absolutely indifferent as how my blunders in the class room affected the students, or how much further they affected the principal or the head teacher. As I mentioned before, I am not a fellow of much audacity to speak of, but I am quick to give up anything when I see its finish.

I had resolved to go elsewhere at once if the school did not suit me. In consequence, neither Badger nor Red Shirt wielded any influence over me. And still less did I feel like coaxing or coddling the youngsters in the class room.

So far it was O. K. with the school, but not so easy as that at my boarding house. I could have stood it if it had been only the boss coming to my room after my tea. But he would fetch many things to my room. First time he brought in seals.* He displayed about ten of them before me and persuaded me to buy them for three yen, which was very cheap, he said. Did he take me for a third rate painter making a round of the country? I told him I did not want them. Next time he brought in a panel picture of flowers and birds, drawn by one Kazan or somebody. He hung it against the wall of the alcove and asked me if it was not well done, and I echoed it looked well done. Then he started lecturing about Kazan, that there are two Kazans, one is Kazan something and the other is Kazan anything, and that this picture was the work of that Kazan something. After this nonsensical lecture, he insisted that he would make it fifteen yen for me to buy it. I declined the offer saying that I was shy of the money.

"You can pay any time. He was insistent. I settled him by telling him of my having no intention of purchasing it even if I had the necessary money. Again next time, he yanked in a big writing stone slab about the size of a ridge-tile.

"This is a tankei,"† he said. As he "tankei-ed" two or three times, I asked for fun what was a tankei. Right away he commenced lecturing on the subject. "There are the upper, the middle and the lower

---

* Artists have several seals of stone with which to stamp on the picture they draw as a guarantee of their personal work or for identification. The shape and kind of seals are quite a hobby among artists, and sales of exchange are of common occurrence.

† Tankei is the name of a place in China where a certain kind of stone suitable for writing purposes was produced.

stratum in tankei," he said. " Most of tankei slabs to-day are made from the upper stratum," he continued, "but this one is surely from the middle stratum. Look at this 'gan.'* 'Tis certainly rare to have three 'gans' like this. The ink-cake grates smoothly on it. Try it, sir," — and he pushed it towards me. I asked him how much, and he answered that on account of its owner having brought it from China and wishing to sell it as soon as possible, he would make it very cheap, that I could have it for thirty yen. I was sure he was a fool. I seemed to be able to get through the school somehow, but I would soon give out if this "curio siege" kept on long.

Shortly afterwards, I began to get sick of the school. One certain night, while I was strolling about a street named Omachi, I happened to notice a sign of noodles below of which was annotated "Tokyo" in the house next to the post office. I am very fond of noodles. While I was in Tokyo, if I passed by a noodle house and smelled the seasoning spices, I felt uncontrollable temptation to go inside at any cost. Up to this time I had forgotten the noodle on account of mathematics and antique curios, but since I had seen thus the sign of noodles, I could hardly pass it by unnoticed. So availing myself of this opportunity, I went in. It was not quite up to what I had judged by the sight. Since it claimed to follow the Tokyo style, they should have tidied up a little bit about the room. They did not either know Tokyo or have the means, I did not know

---

* "Gan" may be understood as a kind of natural mark on the stone peculiar to the stone from Tankei.

which, but the room was miserably dirty. The floor-mats had all seen better days and felt shaggy with sandy dust. The soot-covered walls defied the blackest black. The ceiling was not only smoked by the lamp black, but was so low as to force one involuntarily to bend down his neck. Only the price-list, on which was glaringly written "Noodles" and which was pasted on the wall, was entirely new. I was certain that they bought an old house and opened the business just two or three days before. At the head of the price-list appeared "tempura" (noodles served with shrimp fried in batter).

"Say, fetch me some tempura," I ordered in a loud voice. Then three fellows who had been making a chewing noise together in a corner, looked in my direction. As the room was dark I did not notice them at first. But when we looked at each other, I found them all to be boys in our school. They "how d'ye do'd" me and I acknowledged it. That night, having come across the noodle after so long a time, it tasted so fine that I ate four bowls. The next day as I entered the class room quite unconcernedly, I saw on the black board written in letters so large as to take up the whole space; "Professor Tempura." The boys all glanced at my face and made merry hee-haws at my cost. It was so absurd that I asked them if it was in any way funny for me to eat tempura noodle. Thereupon one of them said, "But four bowls is too much." What did they care if I ate four bowls or five as long as I paid it with my own money, — and speedily finishing up my class, I returned to the teachers' room. After ten minutes' recess, I went to the next class, and there on the black board was newly written quite as large as before; "Four bowls of tempura noodles, but don't laugh."

The first one did not arouse any ill temper in me, but this time it made me feel irritating mad. A joke carried too far becomes mischievous. It is like the undue jealousy of some women who, like coal, look black and suggest flames. No body likes it. These country simpletons, unable to differentiate upon so delicate a boundary, would seem to be bent on pushing everything to the limit. As they lived in such a narrow town where one has no more to see if he goes on strolling about for one hour, and as they were capable of doing nothing better, they were trumpeting aloud this tempura incident in quite as serious a manner as the Russo-Japanese war. What a bunch of miserable pups! It is because they are raised in this fashion from their boyhood that there are many punies who, like the dwarf maple tree in the flower pot, mature gnarled and twisted. I have no objection to laugh myself with others over innocent jokes. But how's this? Boys as they are, they showed a "poisonous temper." Silently erasing off "tempura" from the board, I questioned them if they thought such mischief interesting, that this was a cowardly joke and if they knew the meaning of "cowardice." Some of them answered that to get angry on being laughed at over one's own doing, was cowardice. What made them so disgusting as this! I pitied myself for coming from far off Tokyo to teach such a lot.

"Keep your mouth shut, and study hard," I snapped, and started the class. In the next class again there was written; "When one eats tempura noodles it makes him drawl nonsense." There seemed no end to it. I was thoroughly aroused with anger, and declaring that I would not teach such sassies, went home straight. The boys were glad of having an unexpected holiday, so I heard. When things had come to this pass, the antique curios seemed far more preferable to the school.

My return home and sleep over night greatly rounded off my rugged temper over the tempura affair. I went to the school, and they were there also. I could not tell what was what. The three days thereafter were pacific, and on the night of the fourth day, I went to a suburb called Sumida and ate "dango" (small balls made of glutinous rice, dressed with sugar-paste). Sumida is a town where there are restaurants, hot-springs bath houses and a park, and in addition, the "tenderloin." The dango shop where I went was near the entrance to the tenderloin, and as the dango served there was widely known for its nice taste, I dropped in on my way back from my bath. As I did not meet any students this time I thought nobody knew of it, but when I entered the first hour class next day, I found written on the black board; "Two dishes of dango — 7 sen." It is true that I ate two dishes and paid seven sen. Troublesome kids! I declare. I expected with certainty that there would be something at the second hour, and there it was; "The dango in the tenderloin taste fine." Stupid wretches!

No sooner I thought the dango incident closed than the red towel became the topic for wide spread gossip. Inquiry as to the story revealed it to be something unusually absurd. Since my arrival here, I had made it a part of my routine to take in the hot springs bath every day. While there was nothing in this town which compared favorably with Tokyo, the hot springs were worthy of praise. So long as I was in the town, I decided that I would have a dip every day, and went there walking, partly for physical exercise, before my supper. And whenever I went there I used to carry a large-size European towel dangling from my hand. Added to somewhat reddish color the towel had acquired by its having been soaked in the hot-springs, the red color on its border, which was not fast enough, streaked about so that the towel now looked as if it were dyed red. This towel hung down from my hand on both ways whether afoot or riding in the train. For this reason, the students nicknamed me Red Towel. Honest, it is exasperating to live in a little town.

There is some more. The bath house I patronized was a newly built three-story house, and for the patrons of the first class the house provided a bathrobe, in addition to an attendant, and the cost was only eight sen. On top of that, a maid would serve tea in a regular polite fashion. I always paid the first class. Then those gossipy spotters started saying that for one who made only forty yen a month to take a first class bath every day was extravagant. Why the devil should they care? It was none of their business.

There is still some more. The bath-tub, — or the tank in this case, — was built of granite, and measured about thirty square feet. Usually there were thirteen or fourteen people in the tank, but sometimes there was none. As the water came up clear to the breast, I enjoyed, for athletic purposes, swimming in the tank. I delighted in swimming in this 30-square feet tank, taking chances of the total absence of other people. Once, going downstairs from the third story with a light heart, and peeping through the entrance of the tank to see if I should be able to swim, I noticed a sign put up in which was boldly written; "No swimming allowed in the tank." As there may not have been many who swam in the tank, this notice was probably put up particularly for my sake. After that I gave up swimming. But although I gave up swimming, I was surprised, when I went to the school, to see on the board, as usual, written; "No swimming allowed in the tank." It seemed as if all the students united in tracking me everywhere. They made me sick. I was not a fellow to stop doing whatever I had started upon no matter what students might say, but I became thoroughly disgusted when I meditated on why I had come to such a narrow, suffocating place. And, then, when I returned home, the "antique curio siege" was still going on.

CHAPTER IV.

FOR us teachers there was a duty of night watch in the school, and we had to do it in turn. But Badger and Red Shirt were not in it. On asking why these two were exempt from this duty, I was told that they were accorded by the government treatment similar to officials of "Sonin" rank. Oh, fudge! They were paid more, worked less, and were then excused from this night watch. It was not fair. They made regulations to suit their convenience and seemed to regard all this as a matter of course. How could they be so brazen faced as this! I was greatly dissatisfied relative to this question, but according to the opinion of Porcupine, protests by a single person, with what insistency they may be made, will not be heard. They ought to be heard whether they are made by one person or by two if they are just. Porcupine remonstrated with me by quoting "Might is right" in English. I did not catch his point, so I asked him again, and he told me that it meant the right of the stronger. If it was the right of the stronger I had known it for long, and did not require Porcupine explain that to me at this time. The right of the stronger was a question different from that of the night watch. Who would agree that Badger and Red Shirt were the stronger? But argument or no argument, the turn of this night watch at last fell upon me. Being quite fastidious, I never enjoyed sound sleep unless I slept comfortably in my own bedding. From my childhood, I never stayed out overnight. When I did not find sleeping under the roof of my friends inviting, night watch in the school, you may be sure, was still worse. However repulsive, if this was a part of the forty yen a month, there was no alternative. I had to do it.

To remain alone in the school after the faculty and students had gone home, was something particularly awkward. The room for the night watch was in the rear of the school building at the west end of the dormitory. I stepped inside to see how it was, and finding it squarely facing the setting sun, I thought I would melt. In spite of autumn having already set in, the hot spell still lingered, quite in keeping with the dilly-dally atmosphere of the country. I ordered the same kind of meal as served for the students, and finished my supper. The meal was unspeakably poor. It was a wonder they could subsist on such miserable stuff and keep on "roughing it" in that lively fashion. Not only that, they were always hungry for supper, finishing it at 4.30 in the afternoon. They must be heroes in a sense. I had thus my supper, but the sun being still high, could not go to bed yet. I felt like going to the hot springs. I did not know the wrong or right of night watch going out, but it was oppressively trying to stand a life akin to heavy imprisonment. When I called at the school the first time and inquired about night watch, I was told by the janitor that he had just gone out and I thought it strange. But now by taking the turn of night watch myself, I could fathom the situation; it was right for any night watch to go out. I told the janitor that I was going out for a minute. He asked me "on business?" and I answered "No," but to take a bath at the hot springs, and went out straight. It was too bad that I had left my red towel at home, but I would borrow one over there for to-day.

I took plenty of time in dipping in the bath and as it became dark at last, I came to the Furumachi Station on a train. It was only about four blocks to the school; I could cover it in no time. When I started walking schoolwards, Badger was seen coming from the opposite direction. Badger, I presumed, was going to the hot springs by this train. He came with brisk steps, and as we passed by, I nodded my courtesy. Then Badger, with a studiously owlish countenance, asked:

"Am I wrong to understand that you are night watch?"

Chuck that "Am-I-wrong-to-understand"! Two hours ago, did he not say to me "You're on first night watch to-night. Now, take care of yourself?" What makes one use such a round-about, twisted way of saying anything when he becomes a principal? I was far from smiling.

"Yes, Sir," I said, "I'm night watch tonight, and as I am night watch I will return to the school and stay there overnight, sure." With this parting shot, I left him where we met. Coming then to the cross-streets of Katamachi, I met Porcupine. This is a narrow place, I tell you. Whenever one ventures out, he is sure to come across some familiar face.

"Say, aren't you night watch?" he hallooed, and I said "Yes, I am." "Tis wrong for night watch to leave his post at his pleasure," he added, and to this I blurted out with a bold front; "Nothing wrong at all. It is wrong not to go out."

"Say, old man, your slap-dash is going to the limit. "Wouldn't look well for the principal or the head teacher to see you out like this."

The submissive tone of his remark was contrary to Porcupine as I had known him so far, so I cut him short by saying:

"I have met the principal just now. Why, he approved my taking a stroll about the town. Said it would be hard on night watch unless he took a walk when it is hot." Then I made a bee-line for the school.

Soon it was night. I called the janitor to my room and had a chat for about two hours. I grew tired of this, and thought I would get into bed anyway, even if I could not sleep. I put on my night shirt, lifted the mosquito-net, rolled off the red blanket and fell down flat on my back with a bang. The making of this bumping noise when I go to bed is my habit from my boyhood. "It is a bad habit," once declared a student of a law school who lived on the ground floor, and I on the second, when I was in the boarding house at Ogawa-machi, Kanda-ku, and who brought complaints to my room in person. Students of law schools, weaklings as they are, have double the ability of ordinary persons when it comes to talking. As this student of law dwelt long on absurd accusations, I downed him by answering that the noise made when I went to bed was not the fault of my hip, but that of the house which was not built on a solid base, and that if he had any fuss to make, make it to the house, not to me. This room for night watch was not on the second floor, so nobody cared how much I banged. I do not feel well-rested unless I go to bed with the loudest bang I can make.

"This is bully!" and I straightened out my feet, when something jumped and clung to them. They felt coarse, and seemed not to be fleas. I was a bit surprised, and shook my feet inside the blanket two or three times. Instantly the blamed thing increased, — five or six of them on my legs, two or three on the thighs, one crushed beneath my hip and another clear up to my belly. The shock became greater. Up I jumped, took off the blanket, and about fifty to sixty grasshoppers flew out. I was more or less uneasy until I found out what they were, but now I saw they were grasshoppers, they set me on the war path. "You insignificant grasshoppers, startling a man! See what's coming to you!" With this I slapped them with my pillow twice or thrice, but the objects being so small, the effect was out of proportion to the force with which the blows were administered. I adopted a different plan. In the manner of heating floor-mats with rolled matting at house-cleaning, I sat up in bed and began beating them with the pillow. Many of them flew up by the force of the pillow; some desperately clung on or shot against my nose or head. I could not very well hit those on my head with the pillow; I grabbed such, and dashed them on the floor. What was more provoking was that no matter how hard I dashed them, they landed on the mosquito-net where they made a fluffy jerk and remained, far from being dead. At last, in about half an hour the slaughter of the grasshoppers was ended. I fetched a broom and swept them out. The janitor came along and asked what was the matter.

"Damn the matter! Where in thunder are the fools who keep grasshoppers in bed! You pumpkin-head!"

The janitor answered by explaining that he did not know anything about it. "You can't get away with

Did-not-know," and I followed this thundering by throwing away the broom. The awe-struck janitor shouldered the broom and faded away.

At once I summoned three of the students to my room as the "representatives," and six of them reported. Six or ten made no difference; I rolled up the sleeves of my night-shirt and fired away.

"What do you mean by putting grasshoppers in my bed!"

"Grasshoppers? What are they?" said one in front, in a tone disgustingly quiet. In this school, not only the principal, but the students as well, were addicted to using twisted-round expressions.

"Don't know grasshoppers! You shall see!" To my chagrin, there was none; I had swept them all out. I called the janitor again and told him to fetch those grasshoppers he had taken away. The janitor said he had thrown them into the garbage box, but that he would pick them out again. "Yes, hurry up," I said, and he sped away. After a while he brought back about ten grasshoppers on a white paper, remarking:

"I'm sorry, Sir. It's dark outside and I can't find out more. I'll find some tomorrow." All fools here, down to the janitor. I showed one grasshopper to the students.

"This is a grasshopper. What's the matter for as big idiots as you not to know a grasshopper."

Then the one with a round face sitting on the left saucily shot back: "A-ah say, that's a locust, a-ah ——".

"Shut up. They're the same thing. In the first place, what do you mean by answering your teacher 'A-ah say'? Ah-Say or Ah-Sing is a Chink's name! "

For this counter-shot, he answered: "A-ah say and

Ah-Sing is different, — A-ah say." They never got rid of "Aah say."

"Grasshoppers or locusts, why did you put them into my bed? When I asked you to?"

"Nobody put them in."

"If not, how could they get into the bed?"

"Locusts are fond of warm places and probably they got in there respectfully by themselves,"

"You fools! Grasshoppers getting into bed respectfully! I should smile at them getting in there respectfully! Now, what's the reason for doing this mischief? Speak out."

"But there is no way to explain it because we didn't do it."

Shrimps! If they were afraid of making a clean breast of their own deed, they should not have done it at all. They looked defiant, and appeared to insist on their innocence as long as no evidence was brought up. I myself did some mischief while in the middle school, but when the culprit was sought after, I was never so cowardly, not even once, to back out. What one has done, has been done; what he has not, has not been, — that's the black and white of it. I, for one have been game and square, no matter low much mischief I might have done. If I wished to dodge the punishment, I would not start it. Mischief and punishment are bound to go together. We can enjoy mischief-making with some show of spirit because it is accompanied by certain consequences. Where does one expect to see the dastardly spirit which hungers for mischief-making without punishment, in vogue? The fellows who like to borrow money but not pay it back, are surely such as these students here after they are graduated. What did these fellows come to this middle school for, anyway? They enter a school, tattle round lies, play silly jokes behind some one by sneaking and cheating and get wrongly swell-headed when they finish the school thinking they have received an education. A common lot of jackasses they are.

My hatred of talking with these scamps became intense, so I dismissed them by saying:

"If you fellows have nothing to say, let it go at that. You deserve pity for not knowing the decent from the vulgar after coming to a middle school."

I am not very decent in my own language or manner, but am sure that my moral standard is far more decent than that of these gangs. Those six boys filed out leisurely. Outwardly they appeared more dignified than I their teacher. It was the more repulsive for their calm behavior. I have no temerity equal to theirs. Then I went to bed again, and found the inside of the net full of merry crowds of mosquitoes. I could not bother myself to burn one by one with a candle flame. So I took the net off the hooks, folded it the lengthwise, and shook it crossways, up and down the room. One of the rings of the net, flying round, accidentally hit the back of my hand, the effect of which I did not soon forget. When I went to bed for the third time, I cooled off a little, but could not sleep easily. My watch showed it was half past ten. Well, as I thought it over, I realized myself as having come to a dirty pit. If all teachers of middle schools everywhere have to handle fellows like these in this school, those teachers have my sympathy. It is wonderful that teachers never run short. I believe there are many boneheads of extraordinary patience; but me for something else. In this respect, Kiyo is worthy of admiration. She is an old woman, with neither education nor social position, but as a human, she does more to command our respect. Until now, I have been a trouble to her without appreciating her goodness, but having come alone to such a far-off country, I now appreciated, for the first time, her kindness. If she is fond of sasa-ame of Echigo province, and if I go to Echigo for the purpose of buying that sweetmeat to let her eat it, she is fully worth that trouble. Kiyo has been praising me as unselfish and straight, but she is a person of sterling qualities far more than I whom she praises. I began to feel like meeting her.

While I was thus meditating about Kiyo, all of a sudden, on the floor above my head, about thirty to forty people, if I guess by the number, started stamping the floor with bang, bang, bang that well threatened to bang down the floor. This was followed by proportionately loud whoops. The noise surprised me, and I popped up. The moment I got up I became aware that the students were starting a rough house to get even with me. What wrong one has committed, he has to confess, or his offence is never atoned for. They are just to ask for themselves what crimes they have done. It should be proper that they repent their folly after going to bed and to come and beg me pardon the next morning. Even if they could not go so far as to apologize, they should have kept quiet. Then what does this racket mean? Were we keeping hogs in our dormitory?

"This crazy thing got to stop. See what you get!"

I ran out of the room in my night shirt, and flew upstairs in three and half steps. Then, strange to say, the thunderous rumbling, which I was sure of hearing in the act, was hushed. Not only a whisper but even foot-steps were not heard. This was funny. The lamp was already blown out and although I could not see what was what in the dark, nevertheless could tell by instinct whether there was somebody around or not. In the long corridor running from the east to the west, there was not hiding even a mouse. From other end of the corridor the moonlight flooded in and about there it was particularly light. The scene was somewhat uncanny. I have had the habit from my boyhood of frequently dreaming and of flying out of bed and of muttering things which nobody understood, affording everybody a hearty laugh. One night, when I was sixteen or seventeen, I dreamed that I picked up a diamond, and getting up, demanded of my brother who was sleeping close to me what he had done with that diamond. The demand was made with such force that for about three days all in the house chaffed me about the fatal loss of precious stone, much to my humiliation. Maybe this noise which I heard was but a dream, although I was sure it was real. I was wondering thus in the middle of the corridor, when at the further end where it was moon-lit, a roar was raised, coming from about thirty or forty throats, "One, two, three, — Whee-ee!" The roar had hardly subsided, when, as before, the stamping of the floor commenced with furious rhythm. Ah, it was not a dream, but a real thing!

"Quit making the noise! 'Tis midnight!"

I shouted to beat the band, and started in their direction. My passage was dark; the moonlight yonder was only my guide. About twelve feet past, I stumbled squarely against some hard object; ere the "Ouch!" has passed clear up to my head, I was thrown down. I called all kinds of gods, but could not run. My mind urged me on to hurry up, but my leg would not obey the command. Growing impatient, I hobbled on one foot, and found both voice and stamping already ceased and perfectly quiet. Men can be cowards but I never expected them capable of becoming such dastardly cowards as this. They challenged hogs.

Now the situation having developed to this pretty mess, I would not give it up until I had dragged them out from hiding and forced them to apologize. With this determination, I tried to open one of the doors and examine inside, but it would not open. It was locked or held fast with a pile of tables or something; to my persistent efforts the door stood unyielding. Then I tried one across the corridor on the north side, but it was also locked. While this irritating attempt at door-opening was going on, again on the east end of the corridor the whooping roar and rhythmic stamping of feet were heard. The fools at both ends were bent on making a goose of me. I realized this, but then I was at a loss what to do. I frankly confess that I have not quite as much tact as dashing spirit. In such a case I am wholly at the mercy of swaying circumstances without my own way of getting through it. Nevertheless, I do not expect to play the part of underdog. If I dropped the affair then and there, it would reflect upon my dignity. It would be mortifying to have them think that they had one on the Tokyo kid and that Tokyo-kid was wanting in tenacity. To have it on record that I had been guyed by these in-significant spawn when on night watch, and had to give in to their impudence because I could not handle them, — this would be an indelible disgrace on my life. Mark ye, I am descendant of a samurai of the "hatamoto" class. The blood of the "hatamoto" samurai could be traced to Mitsunaka Tada, who in turn could claim still a nobler ancestor. I am different from, and nobler than, these manure-smelling louts. The only pity is that I am rather short of tact; that I do not know what to do in such a case. That is the trouble. But I would not throw up the sponge; not on your life! I only do not know how because I am honest. Just think, — if the honest does not win, what else is there in this world that will win? If I cannot beat them to-night, I will tomorrow; if not tomorrow, then the day after tomorrow. If not the day after tomorrow, I will sit down right here, get my meals from my home until I beat them.

Thus, resolved, I squatted in the middle of the corridor and waited for the dawn. Myriads of mosquitoes swarmed about me, but I did not mind them. I felt my leg where I hit it a while ago; it seemed bespattered with something greasy. I thought it was bleeding. Let it bleed all it cares! Meanwhile, exhausted by these unwonted affairs, I fell asleep. When I awoke, up I jumped with a curse. The door on my right was half opened, and two students were standing in front of me. The moment I recovered my senses from the drowsy lull, I grabbed a leg of one of them nearest to me, and yanked it with all my might. He fell down prone. Look at what you're getting now! I flew at the other fellow, who was much confused;

gave him vigorous shaking twice or thrice, and he only kept open his bewildering eyes.

"Come up to my room." Evidently they were mollycoddles, for they obeyed my command with out a murmur. The day had become already clear.

I began questioning those two in my room, but, — you cannot pound out the leopard's spots no matter how you may try, — they seemed determined to push it through by an insistent declaration of "not guilty," that they would not confess. While this questioning was going on, the students upstairs came down, one by one, and began congregating in my room. I noticed all their eyes were swollen from want of sleep.

"Blooming nice faces you got for not sleeping only one night. And you call yourselves men! Go, wash your face and come back to hear what I've got to tell you."

I hurled this shot at them, but none of them went to wash his face. For about one hour, I had been talking and back-talking with about fifty students when suddenly Badger put in his appearance. I heard afterward that the janitor ran to Badger for the purpose of reporting to him that there was a trouble in the school. What a weak knee of the janitor to fetch the principal for so trifling an affair as this! No wonder he cannot see better times than a janitor.

The principal listened to my explanation, and also to brief remarks from the students. "Attend school as usual till further notice. Hurry up with washing your face and breakfast; there isn't much time left." So the principal let go all the students. Decidedly slow way of handling, this. If I were the principal, I would expel them right away. It is because the school accords them such luke-warm treatment that they get "fresh" and start "guying" the night watch. He said to me that it must have been trying on my nerves, and that I might be tired, and also that I need not teach that day. To this I replied: "No, Sir, no worrying at all. Such things may happen every night, but it would not disturb me in the least as long I as breathe. I will do the teaching. If I were not able to teach on account of lack of sleep for only one single night, I would make a rebate of my salary to the school."

I do not know how this impressed him, but he gazed at me for a while, and called my attention to the fact that my face was rather swollen. Indeed, I felt it heavy. Besides, it itched all over. I was sure the mosquitoes must have stung me there to their hearts' content. I further added:

"My face may be swollen, but I can talk all right; so I will teach;" thus scratching my face with some warmth. The principal smiled and remarked, "Well, you have the strength." To tell the truth, he did not intend the remark to be a compliment, but, I think, a sneer.

CHAPTER V.

"WON'T you go fishing?" asked Red Shirt. He talks in a strangely womanish voice. One would not be able to tell whether he was a man or a woman. As a man he should talk like one. Is he not a college graduate? I can talk man like enough, and am a graduate from a school of physics at that. It is a shame for a B. A. to have such a squeak.

I answered with the smallest enthusiasm, whereupon he further asked me an impolite question if I ever did fishing. I told him not much, that I once caught three gibels when I was a boy, at a fishing game pond at Koume, and that I also caught a carp about eight inches long, at a similar game at the festival of Bishamon at Kagurazaka; — the carp, just as I was coaxing it out of the water, splashed back into it, and when I think of the incident I feel mortified at the loss even now. Red Shirt stuck out his chin and laughed "ho, ho." Why could he not laugh just like an ordinary person? "Then you are not well acquainted with the spirit of the game," he cried.. "I'll show you if you like." He seemed highly elated.

Not for me! I take it this way that generally those who are fond of fishing or shooting have cruel hearts. Otherwise, there is no reason why they could derive pleasure in murdering innocent creatures. Surely, fish and birds would prefer living to getting killed. Except those who make fishing or shooting their calling, it is nonsense for those who are well off to say that they cannot sleep well unless they seek the lives of fish or birds. This was the way I looked at the question, but as he was a B. A. and would have a better command of language when it came to talking, I kept mum, knowing he would beat me in argument. Red Shirt mistook my silence for my surrender, and began to induce me to join him right away, saying he would show me some fish and I should come with him if I was not busy, because he and Mr. Yoshikawa were lonesome when alone. Mr. Yoshikawa is the teacher of drawing whom I had nicknamed Clown. I don't know what's in the mind of this Clown, but he was a constant visitor at the house of Red Shirt, and wherever he went, Clown was sure to be trailing after him. They appeared more like master and servant than two fellow teachers. As Clown used to follow Red Shirt like a shadow, it would be natural to see them go off together now, but when those two alone would have been well off, why should they invite me, — this brusque, unaesthetic fellow, — was hard to understand. Probably, vain of his fishing ability, he desired to show his skill, but he aimed at the wrong mark, if that was his intention, as nothing of the kind would touch me. I would not be chagrined if he fishes out two or three tunnies. I am a man myself, and poor though I may be in the art, I would hook something if I dropped a line. If I declined his invitation, Red Shirt would suspect that I refused not because of my lack of interest in the game but because of my want of skill of fishing. I weighed the matter thus, and accepted his invitation. After the school, I returned home and got ready, and having joined Red Shirt and Clown at the station, we three started to the shore. There was only one boatman to row; the boat was long and narrow, a kind we do not have in Tokyo. I looked for fishing rods but could find none.

"How can we fish without rods? How are we going to manage it?" I asked Clown and he told me with the air of a professional fisherman that no rods were needed in the deep-sea fishing, but only lines. I had better not asked him if I was to be talked down in this way.

The boatman was rowing very slowly, but his skill was something wonderful. We had already come far out to sea, and on turning back, saw the shore minimized, fading in far distance. The five-storied pagoda of Tosho Temple appeared above the surrounding woods like a needle-point. Yonder stood Aoshima (Blue Island). Nobody was living on this island which a closer view showed to be covered with stones and pine trees. No wonder no one could live there. Red Shirt was intently surveying about and praising the general view as fine. Clown also termed it "an absolutely fine view." I don't know whether it is so fine as to be absolute, but there was no doubt as to the exhilarating air. I realized it as the best tonic to be thus blown by the fresh sea breeze upon a wide expanse of water. I felt hungry.

"Look at that pine; its trunk is straight and spreads its top branches like an umbrella. Isn't it a Turneresque picture?" said Red Shirt. "Yes, just like Turner's," responded Clown, "Isn't the way it curves just elegant? Exactly the touch of Turner," he added with some show of pride. I didn't know what Turner was, but as I could get along without knowing it, I kept silent. The boat turned to the left with the island on the right. The sea was so perfectly calm as to tempt one to think he was not on the deep sea. The pleasant occasion was a credit to Red Shirt. As I wished, if possible, to land on the island, I asked the boatman if our boat could not be made to it. Upon this Red Shirt objected, saying that we could do so but it was not advisable to go too close the shore for fishing. I kept still for a while. Then Clown made the unlooked-for proposal that the island be named Turner Island. "That's good. We shall call it so hereafter," seconded Red Shirt. If I was included in that "We," it was something I least cared for. Aoshima was good enough for me. "By the way, how would it look," said Clown, "if we place Madonna by Raphael upon that rock? It would make a fine picture."

"Let's quit talking about Madonna, ho, ho, ho," and Red Shirt emitted a spooky laugh.

"That's all right. Nobody's around," remarked Clown as he glanced at me, and turning his face to the other direction significantly, smiled devilishly. I felt sickened.

As it was none of my business whether it was a Madonna or a kodanna (young master), they let pose there any old way, but it was vulgar to feign assurance that one's subject is in no danger of being understood so long as others did not know the subject. Clown claims himself as a Yedo kid. I thought that the person called Madonna was no other than a favorite geisha of Red Shirt. I should smile at the idea of his gazing at his tootsy-wootsy standing beneath a pine tree. It would be better if Clown would make an oil painting of the scene and exhibit it for the public.

"This will be about the best place." So saying the boatman stopped rowing the boat and dropped an anchor.

"How deep is it?" asked Red Shirt, and was told about six fathoms.

"Hard to fish sea-breams in six fathoms," said Red Shirt as he dropped a line into the water. The old sport appeared to expect to fetch some bream. Bravo!

"It wouldn't be hard for you. Besides it is calm," Clown fawningly remarked, and he too dropped a line. The line had only a tiny bit of lead that looked like a weight. It had no float. To fish without a float seemed as nearly reasonable as to measure the heat without a thermometer, which was something impossible for me. So I looked on. They then told me to start, and asked me if I had any line. I told them I had more than I could use, but that I had no float.

"To say that one is unable to fish without a float shows that he is a novice," piped up Clown.

"See? When the line touches the bottom, you just manage it with your finger on the edge. If a fish bites, you could tell in a minute. There it goes," and Red Shirt hastily started taking out the line. I wondered what he had got, but I saw no fish, only the bait was gone. Ha, good for you, Gov'nur!

"Wasn't it too bad! I'm sure it was a big one. If you miss that way, with your ability, we would have to keep a sharper watch to-day. But, say, even if we miss the fish, it's far better than staring at a float, isn't it? Just like saying he can't ride a bike without a brake." Clown has been getting rather gay, and I was almost tempted to swat him. I'm just as good as they are. The sea isn't leased by Red Shirt, and there might be one obliging bonito which might get caught by my line. I dropped my line then, and toyed it with my finger carelessly.

After a while something shook my line with successive jerks. I thought it must be a fish. Unless it was something living, it would not give that tremulous shaking. Good! I have it, and I commenced drawing in the line, while Clown jibed me "What? Caught one already? Very remarkable, indeed!" I had drawn in nearly all the line, leaving only about five feet in the water. I peeped over and saw a fish that looked like a gold fish with stripes was coming up swimming to right and left. It was interesting. On taking it out of the water, it wriggled and jumped, and covered my face with water. After some effort, I had it and tried to detach the hook, but it would not come out easily. My hands became greasy and the sense was anything but pleasing. I was irritated; I swung the line and banged the fish against the bottom of the boat. It speedily died. Red Shirt and Clown watched me with surprise. I washed my hands in the water but they still smelled "fishy." No more for me! I don't care what fish I might get, I don't want to grab a fish. And I presume the fish doesn't want to be grabbed either. I hastily rolled up the line.

"Splendid for the first honor, but that's goruki," Clown again made a "fresh" remark.

"Goruki sounds like the name of a Russian literator," said Red Shirt. "Yes, just like a Russian literator," Clown at once seconded Red Shirt.

Gorky for a Russian literator, Maruki a photographer of Shibaku, and komeno-naruki (rice) a lifegiver, eh? This Red Shirt has a bad hobby of marshalling before anybody the name of foreigners. Everybody has his specialty. How could a teacher of mathematics like me tell whether it is a Gorky or shariki (rikishaman). Red Shirt should have been a little more considerate. And if he wants to mention such names at all, let him mention "Autobiography of Ben Franklin," or "Pushing to the Front," or something we all know. Red Shirt has been seen once in a while bringing a magazine with a red cover entitled Imperial Literature to the school and poring over it with reverence. I heard it from Porcupine that Red Shirt gets his supply of all foreign names from that magazine. Well, I should say!

For some time, Red Shirt and Clown fished assiduously and within about an hour they caught about fifteen fish. The funny part of it was that all they caught were goruki; of sea-bream there was not a sign.

"This is a day of bumper crop of Russian literature," Red Shirt said, and Clown answered:

"When one as skilled as you gets nothing but goruki, it's natural for me to get nothing else."

The boatman told me that this small-sized fish goruki has too many tiny bones and tastes too poor to be fit for eating, but they could be used for fertilising. So Red Shirt and Clown were fishing fertilisers with vim and vigor. As for me, one goruki was enough and I laid down myself on the bottom, and looked up at the sky. This was far more dandy than fishing.

Then the two began whispering. I could not hear well, nor did I care to. I was looking up at the sky and thinking about Kiyo. If I had enough of money, I thought, and came with Kiyo to such a picturesque place, how joyous it would be. No matter how picturesque the scene might be, it would be flat in the company of Clown or of his kind. Kiyo is a poor wrinkled woman, but I am not ashamed to take her to any old place. Clown or his likes, even in a Victoria or a yacht, or in a sky-high position, would not be worthy to come within her shadow. If I were the head teacher, and Red Shirt were I, Clown would be sure to fawn on me and jeer at Red Shirt. They say Yedo kids are flippant. Indeed, if a fellow like Clown was to travel the country and repeatedly declare "I am a Yedo kid," no wonder the country folk would decide that the flippant are Yedo kids and Yedo kids are flippant. While I was meditating like this, I heard suppressed laughter. Between their laughs they talked something, but I could not make out what they were talking about. "Eh? I don't know ......" :...... That's true ...... he doesn't know ...... isn't it pity, though ...." "Can that be ...." "With grasshoppers ...... that's a fact."

I did not listen to what they were talking, but when I heard Clown say "grasshoppers," I cocked my ear instinctively. Clown emphasized, for what reason I do not know the word "grasshoppers" so that it would be sure to reach my ear plainly, and he blurred the rest on purpose. I did not move, and kept on listening. "That same old Hotta," "that may be the case ......" "Tempura ...... ha, ha, ha ......" "...... incited ......" "...... dango also? ......"

The words were thus choppy, but judging by their saying "grasshoppers," "tempura" or "dango," I was sure they were secretly talking something about me. If they wanted to talk, they should do it louder. If they wanted to discuss something secret, why in thunder did they invite me? What damnable blokes! Grasshoppers or glass-stoppers, I was not in the wrong; I have kept quiet to save the face of Badger because the principle asked me to leave the matter to him. Clown has been making unnecessary criticisms; out with your old paint-brushes there! Whatever concerns me, I will settle it myself sooner or later, and they had just to keep off my toes. But remarks such as "the same old Hotta" or "...... incited ......" worried me a bit. I could not make out whether they meant that Hotta incited me to extend the circle of the trouble, or that he incited the students to get at me. As I gazed at the blue sky, the sunlight gradually waned and chilly winds commenced stirring. The clouds that resembled the streaky smokes of joss sticks were slowly extending over a clear sky, and by degrees they were absorbed, melted and changed to a faint fog.

"Well, let's be going," said Red Shirt suddenly. "Yes, this is the time we were going. See your Madonna to-night?" responded Clown. "Cut out nonsense ...... might mean a serious trouble," said Red Shirt who was reclining against the edge of the boat, now raising himself. "O, that's all right if he hears ....," and when Clown, so saying, turned himself my way, I glared squarely in his face. Clown turned back as if to keep away from a dazzling light, and with "Ha, this is going some," shrugged his shoulders and scratched his head.

The boat was now being rowed shore-ward over the calm sea. "You don't seem much fond of fishing," asked Red Shirt. "No, I'd rather prefer lying and looking at the sky," I answered, and threw the stub of cigarette I had been smoking into the water; it sizzled and floated on the waves parted by the oar.

"The students are all glad because you have come. So we want you do your best." Red Shirt this time started something quite alien to fishing. "I don't think they are," I said. "Yes; I don't mean it as flattery. They are, sure. Isn't it so, Mr. Yoshikawa?"

"I should say they are. They're crazy over it," said Clown with an unctuous smile. Strange that whatever Clown says, it makes me itching mad. "But, if you don't look out, there is danger," warned Red Shirt.

"I am fully prepared for all dangers," I replied. In fact, I had made up my mind either to get fired or to make all the students in the dormitory apologize to me.

"If you talk that way, that cuts everything out. Really, as a head teacher, I've been considering what is good for you, and wouldn't like you to mistake it."

"The head teacher is really your friend. And I'm doing what I can for you, though mighty little, because you and I are Yedo kids, and I would like to have you stay with us as long as possible and we can help each other." So said Clown and it sounded almost human. I would sooner hang myself than to get helped by Clown.

"And the students are all glad because you had come, but there are many circumstances," continued Red Shirt. "You may feel angry sometimes but be patient for the present, and I will never do anything to hurt your interests."

"You say 'many circumstances'; what are they?"

"They're rather complicated. Well, they'll be clear to you by and by. You'll understand them naturally without my talking them over. What do you say, Mr. Yoshikawa?"

"Yes, they're pretty complicated; hard to get them cleared up in a jiffy. But they'll become clear by-the-bye. Will be understood naturally without my explaining them," Clown echoed Red Shirt.

"If they're such a bother, I don't mind not hearing them. I only asked you because you sprang the subject."

"That's right. I may seem irresponsible in not concluding the thing I had started. Then this much I'll tell you. I mean no offense, but you are fresh from school, and teaching is a new experience. And a school is a place where somewhat complicated private circumstances are common and one cannot do everything straight and simple".

"If can't get it through straight and simple, how does it go?"

"Well, there you are so straight as that. As I was saying, you're short of experience ......"

"I should be. As I wrote it down in my record-sheet, I'm 23 years and four months."

"That's it. So you'd be done by some one in unexpected quarter."

"I'm not afraid who might do me as long as I'm honest."

"Certainly not. No need be afraid, but I do say you look sharp; your predecessor was done."

I noticed Clown had become quiet, and turning round, saw him at the stern talking with the boatman. Without Clown, I found our conversation running smoothly.

"By whom was my predecessor done?"

"If I point out the name, it would reflect on the honor of that person, so I can't mention it. Besides there is no evidence to prove it and I may be in a bad fix if I say it. At any rate, since you're here, my efforts will prove nothing if you fail. Keep a sharp lookout, please."

"You say lookout, but I can't be more watchful than I am now. If I don't do anything wrong, after all, that's all right isn't it?"

Red Shirt laughed. I did not remember having said anything provocative of laughter. Up to this very minute, I have been firm in my conviction that I'm right. When I come to consider the situation, it appears that a majority of people are encouraging others to become bad. They seem to believe that one must do wrong in order to succeed. If they happen to see some one honest and pure, they sneer at him as "Master Darling" or "kiddy." What's the use then of the instructors of ethics at grammar schools or middle schools teaching children not to tell a lie or to be honest. Better rather make a bold departure and teach at schools the gentle art of lying or the trick of distrusting others, or show pupils how to do others. That would be beneficial for the person thus taught and for the public as well. When Red Shirt laughed, he laughed at my simplicity. My word! what chances have the simple-hearted or the pure in a society where they are made objects of contempt! Kiyo would never laugh at such a time; she would listen with profound respect. Kiyo is far superior to Red Shirt.

"Of course, that's all right as long as you don't do anything wrong. But although you may not do anything wrong, they will do you just the same unless you can see the wrong of others. There are fellows you have got to watch, — the fellows who may appear off-hand, simple and so kind as to get boarding house for you ...... Getting rather cold. 'Tis already autumn, isn't it. The beach looks beer-color in the fog. A fine view. Say, Mr. Yoshikawa, what do you think of the scene along the beach? ......" This in a loud voice was addressed to Clown.

"Indeed, this is a fine view. I'd get a sketch of it if I had time. Seems a pity to leave it there," answered Clown.

A light was seen upstairs at Minatoya, and just as the whistle of a train was sounded, our boat pushed its nose deep into the sand. "Well, so you're back early," courtesied the wife of the boatman as she stepped upon the sand. I stood on the edge of the boat; and whoop! I jumped out to the beach.

CHAPTER VI.

I heartily despise Clown. It would be beneficial for Japan if such a fellow were tied to a quernstone and dumped into the sea. As to Red Shirt, his voice did not suit my fancy. I believe he suppresses his natural tones to put on airs and assume genteel manner. He may put on all kinds of airs, but nothing good will come of it with that type of face. If anything falls in love with him, perhaps the Madonna will be about the limit. As a head-teacher, however, he is more serious than Clown. As he did not say definitely, I cannot get to the point, but it appears that he warned me to look-out for Porcupine as he is crooked. If that was the case, he should have declared it like a man. And if Porcupine is so bad a teacher as that, it would be better to discharge him. What a lack of backbone for a head teacher and a Bachelor of Arts! As he is a fellow so cautious as to be unable to mention the name of the other even in a whisper, he is surely a mollycoddle. All mollycoddles are kind, and that Red Shirt may be as kind as a woman. His kindness is one thing, and his voice quite another, and it would be wrong to disregard his kindness on account of his voice. But then, isn't this world a funny place! The fellow I don't like is kind to me, and the friend whom I like is crooked, — how absurd! Probably everything here goes in opposite directions as it is in the country, the contrary holds in Tokyo. A dangerous place, this. By degrees, fires may get frozen and custard pudding petrified. But it is hardly believable that Porcupine would incite the students, although he might do most anything he wishes as he is best liked among them. Instead of taking in so roundabout a way, in the first place, it would have saved him a lot of trouble if he came direct to me and got at me for a fight. If I am in his way, he had better tell me so, and ask me to resign because I am in his way. There is nothing that cannot be settled by talking it over. If what he says sounds reasonable, I would resign even tomorrow. This is not the only town where I can get bread and butter; I ought not to die homeless wherever I go. I thought Porcupine was a better sport.

When I came here, Porcupine was the first to treat me to ice water. To be treated by such a fellow, even if it is so trifling a thing as ice water, affects my honor. I had only one glass then and had him pay only one sen and a half. But one sen or half sen, I shall not die in peace if I accept a favor from a swindler. I will pay it back tomorrow when I go to the school. I borrowed three yen from Kiyo. That three yen is not paid yet to-day, though it is five years since. Not that I could not pay, but that I did not want to. Kiyo never looks to my pocket, thinking I shall pay it back by-the-bye. Not by any means. I myself do not expect to fulfill cold obligation like a stranger by meditating on returning it. The more I worry about paying it back, the more I may be doubting the honest heart of Kiyo. It would be the same as traducing her pure mind. I have not paid her back that three yen not because I regard her lightly, but because I regard her as part of myself. Kiyo and Porcupine cannot be compared, of course, but whether it be ice water or tea, the fact that I accept another's favor without saying anything is an act of good-will, taking the other on his par value, as a decent fellow.

Instead of chipping in my share, and settling each account, to receive munificence with grateful mind is an acknowledgment which no amount of money can purchase. I have neither title nor official position but I am an independent fellow, and to have an independent fellow kowtow to you in acknowledgment of the favor you extend him should be considered as far more than a return acknowledgment with a million yen. I made Porcupine blow one sen and a half, and gave him my gratitude which is more costly than a million yen. He ought to have been thankful for that. And then what an outrageous fellow to plan a cowardly action behind my back! I will give him back that one sen and a half tomorrow, and all will be square. Then I will land him one. When I thought thus far, I felt sleepy and slept like a log. The next day, as I had something in my mind, I went to the school earlier than usual and waited for Porcupine, but he did not appear for a considerable time. "Confucius" was there, so was Clown, and finally Red Shirt, but for Porcupine there was a piece of chalk on his desk but the owner was not there. I had been thinking of paying that one sen and a half as soon as I entered the room, and had brought the coppers to the school grasped in my hand. My hands get easily sweaty, and when I opened my hand, I found them wet. Thinking that Porcupine might say something if wet coins were given him, I placed them upon my desk, and cooled them by blowing in them. Then Red Shirt came to me and said he was sorry to detain me yesterday, thought I have been annoyed. I told him I was not annoyed at all, only I was hungry. Thereupon Red Shirt put his elbows upon the desk, brought his sauce-pan-like face close to my nose, and said; "Say, keep dark what I told you yesterday in the boat. You haven't told it anybody, have you?" He seems quite a nervous fellow, as becoming one who talks in a feminish voice. It was certain that I had not told it to anybody, but as I was in the mood to tell it and had already one sen and a half in my hand, I would be a little rattled if a gag was put on me. To the devil with Red Shirt! Although he had not mentioned the name "Porcupine," he had given me such pointers as to put me wise as to who the objective was, and now he requested me not to blow the gaff! — it was an irresponsibility least to be expected from a head teacher. In the ordinary run of things, he should step into the thick of the fight between Porcupine and me, and side with me with all his colors flying. By so doing, he might be worthy the position of the head teacher, and vindicate the principle of wearing red shirts.

I told the head teacher that I had not divulged the secret to anybody but was going to fight it out with Porcupine. Red Shirt was greatly perturbed, and stuttered out; "Say, don't do anything so rash as that. I don't remember having stated anything plainly to you about Mr. Hotta ...... if you start a scrimmage here, I'll be greatly embarrassed." And he asked the strangely outlandish question if I had come to the school to start trouble? Of course not, I said, the school would not stand for my making trouble and pay me salary for it. Red Shirt then, perspiring, begged me to keep the secret as mere reference and never mention it. "All right, then," I assured him, "this robs me shy, but since you're so afraid of it, I'll keep it all to myself." "Are you sure?" repeated

Red Shirt. There was no limit to his womanishness. If Red Shirt was typical of Bachelors of Arts, I did not see much in them. He appeared composed after having requested me to do something self-contradictory and wanting logic, and on top of that suspects my sincerity.

"Don't you mistake," I said to myself, "I'm a man to the marrow, and haven't the idea of breaking my own promises; mark that!"

Meanwhile the occupants of the desks on both my sides came to the room, and Red Shirt hastily withdrew to his own desk. Red Shirt shows some air even in his walk. In stepping about the room, he places down his shoes so as to make no sound. For the first time I came to know that making no sound in one's walk was something satisfactory to one's vanity. He was not training himself for a burglar, I suppose. He should cut out such nonsense before it gets worse. Then the bugle for the opening of classes was heard. Porcupine did not appear after all. There was no other way but to leave the coins upon the desk and attend the class.

When I returned to the room a little late after the first hour class, all the teachers were there at their desks, and Porcupine too was there. The moment Porcupine saw my face, he said that he was late on my account, and I should pay him a fine. I took out that one sen and a half, and saying it was the price of the ice water, shoved it on his desk and told him to take it. "Don't josh me," he said, and began laughing, but as I appeared unusually serious, he swept the coins back to my desk, and flung back, "Quit fooling." So he really meant to treat me, eh?

"No fooling; I mean it," I said. "I have no reason to accept your treat, and that's why I pay you back. Why don't you take it?"

"If you're so worried about that one sen and a half, I will take it, but why do you pay it at this time so suddenly?"

"This time or any time, I want to pay it back. I pay it back because I don't like you treat me."

Porcupine coldly gazed at me and ejaculated "H'm." If I had not been requested by Red Shirt, here was the chance to show up his cowardice and make it hot for him. But since I had promised not to reveal the secret, I could do nothing. What the deuce did he mean by "H'm" when I was red with anger.

"I'll take the price of the ice water, but I want you to leave your boarding house."

"Take that coin; that's all there is to it. To leave or not, — that's my pleasure."

"But that is not your pleasure. The boss of your boarding house came to me yesterday and wanted me to tell you leave the house, and when I heard his explanation, what he said was reasonable. And I dropped there on my way here this morning to hear more details and make sure of everything."

What Porcupine was trying to get at was all dark to me.

"I don't care a snap what the boss was damn well pleased to tell you," I cried. "What do you mean by deciding everything by yourself! If there is any reason, tell me first. What's the matter with you, deciding what the boss says is reasonable without hearing me."

"Then you shall hear," he said. "You're too tough and been regarded a nuisance over there. Say, the wife of a boarding house is a wife, not a maid, and you've been such a four-flusher as to make her wipe your feet."

"When did I make her wipe my feet?" I asked.

"I don't know whether you did or did not, but anyway they're pretty sore about you. He said he can make ten or fifteen yen easily if he sell a roll of panel-picture."

"Damn the chap! Why did he take me for a boarder then!"

"I don't know why. They took you but they want you to leave because they got tired of you. So you'd better get out."

"Sure, I will. Who'd stay in such a house even if they beg me on their knees. You're insolent to have induced me to go to such a false accuser in the first place."

"Might be either I'm insolent or you're tough." Porcupine is no less hot-tempered than I am, and spoke with equally loud voice. All the other teachers in the room, surprised, wondering what has happened, looked in our direction and craned their necks. I was not conscious of having done anything to be ashamed of, so I stood up and looked around. Clown alone was laughing amused. The moment he met my glaring stare as if to say "You too want to fight?" he suddenly assumed a grave face and became serious. He seemed to be a little cowed. Meanwhile the bugle was heard, and Porcupine and I stopped the quarrel and went to the class rooms.

In the afternoon, a meeting of the teachers was going to be held to discuss the question of punishment of those students in the dormitory who offended me the other night. This meeting was a thing I had to attend for the first time in my life, and I was totally ignorant about it. Probably it was where the teachers gathered to blow about their own opinions and the principal bring them to compromise somehow. To compromise is a method used when no decision can be delivered as to the right or wrong of either side. It seemed to me a waste of time to hold a meeting over an affair in which the guilt of the other side was plain as daylight. No matter who tried to twist it round, there was no ground for doubting the facts. It would have been better if the principal had decided at once on such a plain case; he is surely wanting in decision. If all principals are like this, a principal is a synonym of a "dilly-dally."

The meeting hall was a long, narrow room next to that of the principal, and was used for dining room. About twenty chairs, with black leather seat, were lined around a narrow table, and the whole scene looked like a restaurant in Kanda. At one end of the table the principal took his seat, and next to him Red Shirt. All the rest shifted for themselves, but the gymnasium teacher is said always to take the seat farthest down out of modesty. The situation was new to me, so I sat down between the teachers of natural history and of Confucius. Across the table sat Porcupine and Clown. Think how I might, the face of Clown was a degrading type. That of Porcupine was far more charming, even if I was now on bad terms with him. The panel picture which hung in the alcove of the reception hall of Yogen temple where I went to the funeral of my father, looked exactly like this Porcupine. A priest told me the picture was the face of a strange creature called Idaten. To-day he was pretty sore, and frequently stared at me with his fiery eyes rolling. "You can't bulldoze me with that," I thought, and rolled my own in defiance and stared back at him. My eyes are not well-shaped but their large size is seldom beaten by others. Kiyo even once suggested that I should make a fine actor because I had big eyes.

"All now here?" asked the principal, and the clerk named Kawamura counted one, two, three and one was short. "Just one more," said the clerk, and it ought to be; Hubbard Squash was not there. I don't know what affinity there is between Hubbard Squash and me, but I can never forget his face. When I come to the teachers' room, his face attracts me first; while walking out in the street, his manners are recalled to my mind. When I go to the hot springs, some-times I meet him with a pale-face in the bath, and if I hallooed to him, he would raise his trembling head, making me feel sorry for him. In the school there is no teacher so quiet as he. He seldom, if ever, laughs or talks. I knew the word "gentleman" from books, and thought it was found only in the dictionary, but not a thing alive. But since I met Hubbard Squash, I was impressed for the first time that the word rep-resented a real substance.

As he is a man so attached to me, I had noticed his absence as soon as I entered the meeting hall. To tell the truth, I came to the hall with the intention of sitting next to him. The principal said that the ab-sentee may appear shortly, and untied a package he had before him, taking out some hectograph sheets and began reading them. Red Shirt began polishing his amber pipe with a silk handkerchief. This was his hobby, which was probably becoming to him. Others whispered with their neighbors. Still others were writing nothings upon the table with the erasers at the end of their pencils. Clown talked to Porcupine once in a while, but he was not responsive. He only said "Umh" or "Ahm," and stared at me with wrathful eyes. I stared back with equal ferocity.

Then the tardy Hubbard Squash apologetically entered, and politely explained that he was unavoidably detained. "Well, then the meeting is called to order," said Badger. On these sheets was printed, first the question of the punishment of the offending students, second that of superintending the students, and two or three other matters. Badger, putting on airs as usual, as if he was an incarnation of education, spoke to the following effect.

"Any misdeeds or faults among the teachers or the students in this school are due to the lack of virtues in my person, and whenever anything happens, I inwardly feel ashamed that a man like me could hold his position. Unfortunately such an affair has taken place again, and I have to apologize from my heart. But since it has happened, it cannot be helped; we must settle it one way or other. The facts are as you already know, and I ask you gentlemen to state frankly the best means by which the affair may be settled."

When I heard the principal speak, I was impressed that indeed the principal, or Badger, was saying something "grand." If the principal was willing to assume all responsibilities, saying it was his fault or his lack of virtues, it would have been better to stop punishing the students and get himself fired first. Then there will be no need of holding such thing as a meeting. In the first place, just consider it by common sense. I was doing my night duty right, and the students started trouble. The wrong doer is neither the principal nor I. If Porcupine incited them, then it would be enough to get rid of the students and Porcupine. Where in thunder would a peach of damfool be who always swipes other people's faults and says "these are mine?" It was a stunt made possible only by Badger. Having made such an illogical statement, he glanced at the teachers in a highly pleased manner. But no one opened his mouth. The teacher of natural history was gazing at the crow which had hopped on the roof of the nearby building. The teacher of Confucius was folding and unfolding the hectograph sheet. Porcupine was still staring at me. If a meeting was so nonsensical an affair as this, I would have been better absent taking a nap at home.

I became irritated, and half raised myself, intending to make a convincing speech, but just then Red Shirt began saying something and I stopped. I saw him say something, having put away his pipe, and wiping his face with a striped silk handkerchief. I'm sure he copped that handkerchief from the Madonna; men should use white linen. He said:

"When I heard of the rough affairs in the dormitory, I was greatly ashamed as the head teacher of my lack of discipline and influence. When such an affair takes place there is underlying cause somewhere. Looking at the affair itself, it may seem that the students were wrong, but in a closer study of the facts, we may find the responsibility resting with the

School. Therefore, I'm afraid it might affect us badly in the future if we administer too severe a punishment on the strength of what has been shown on the surface. As they are youngsters, full of life and vigor, they might half-consciously commit some youthful pranks, without due regard as to their good or bad. As to the mode of punishment itself, I have no right to suggest since it is a matter entirely in the hand of the principal, but I should ask, considering these points, that some leniency be shown toward the students."

Well, as Badger, so was Red Shirt. He declares the "Rough Necks" among the students is not their fault but the fault of the teachers. A crazy person beats other people because the beaten are wrong. Very grateful, indeed. If the students were so full of life and vigor, shovel them out into the campus and let them wrestle their heads off. Who would have grasshoppers put into his bed unconsciously! If things go on like this, they may stab some one asleep, and get freed as having done the deed unconsciously.

Having figured it out in this wise, I thought I would state my own views on the matter, but I wanted to give them an eloquent speech and fairly take away their breath. I have an affection of the windpipe which clogs after two or three words when I am excited. Badger and Red Shirt are below my standing in their personality, but they were skilled in speech-making, and it would not do to have them see my awkwardness. I'll make a rough note of composition first, I thought, and started mentally making a sentence, when, to my surprise, Clown stood up suddenly. It was unusual for Clown to state his opinion. He spoke in his flippant tone:

"Really the grasshopper incident and the whoop-la affair are peculiar happenings which are enough to make us doubt our own future. We teachers at this time must strive to clear the atmosphere of the school. And what the principal and the head teacher have said just now are fit and proper. I entirely agree with their opinions. I wish the punishment to be moderate."

In what Clown had said there were words but no meaning. It was a juxtaposition of high-flown words making no sense. All that I understood was the words, "I entirely agree with their opinions."

Clown's meaning was not clear to me, but as I was thoroughly angered, I rose without completing my rough note.

"I am entirely opposed to ...." I said, but the rest did not come at once. "....... I don't like such a topsy-turvy settlement," I added and the fellows began laughing. "The students are absolutely wrong from the beginning. It would set a bad precedent if we don't make them apologize .... What do we care if we kick them all out .... darn the kids trying to guy a new comer ...." and I sat down. Then the teacher of natural history who sat on my right whined a weak opinion, saying "The students may be wrong, but if we punish them too severely, they may start a reaction and would make it rather bad. I am for the moderate side, as the head teacher suggested." The teacher of Confucius on my left expressed his agreement with the moderate side, and so did the teacher of history endorse the views of the head teacher. Dash those weak-knees! Most of them belonged to the coterie of Red Shirt. It would make a dandy school if such fellows run it. I had decided in my mind that it must be either the students apologize to me or I resign, and if the opinion of Red Shirt prevailed, I had determined to return home and pack up. I had no ability of out-talking such fellows, or even if I had, I was in no humor to keeping their company for long. Since I don't expect to remain in the school, the devil may take care of the rest. If I said anything, they would only laugh; so I shut my mouth tight.

Porcupine, who up to this time had been listening to the others, stood up with some show of spirit. Ha, the fellow was going to endorse the views of Red Shirt, eh? You and I got to fight it out anyway, I thought, so do any way you darn please. Porcupine spoke in a thunderous voice:

"I entirely differ from the opinions of the head teacher and other gentlemen. Because, viewed from whatever angle, this incident cannot be other than an attempt by those fifty students in the dormitory to make a fool of a new teacher. The head teacher seems to trace the cause of the trouble to the personality of that teacher himself, but, begging his pardon, I think he is mistaken. The night that new teacher was on night duty was not long after his arrival, not more than twenty days after he had come into contact with the students. During those short twenty days, the students could have no reason to criticise his knowledge or his person. If he was insulted for some cause which deserved insult, there may be reasons in our considering the act of the students, but if we show undue leniency toward the frivolous students who would insult a new teacher without cause, it would affect the dignity of this school. The spirit of education is not only in imparting technical knowledge, but also in encouraging honest, ennobling and samurai-like virtues, while eliminating the evil tendency to vulgarity and roughness. If we are afraid of reaction or further trouble, and satisfy ourselves with make-shifts, there is no telling when we can ever get rid of this evil atmosphere. We are here to eradicate this very evil. If we mean to countenance it, we had better not accepted our positions here. For these reasons, I believe it proper to punish the students in the dormitory to the fullest extent and also make them apologize to that teacher in the open."

All were quiet. Red Shirt again began polishing his pipe. I was greatly elated. He spoke almost what I had wanted to. I'm such a simple-hearted fellow that I forgot all about the bickerings with Porcupine, and looked at him with a grateful face, but he appeared to take no notice of me.

After a while, Porcupine again stood up, and said. "I forgot to mention just now, so I wish to add. The teacher on night duty that night seems to have gone to the hot springs during his duty hours, and I think it a blunder. It is a matter of serious misconduct to take the advantage of being in sole charge of the school, to slip out to a hot springs. The bad behavior of the students is one thing; this blunder is another, and I wish the principal to call attention of the re-sponsible person to that matter."

A strange fellow! No sooner had he backed me up than he began talking me down. I knew the other night watch went out during his duty hours, and thought it was a custom, so I went as far out as to the hot springs without considering the situation seriously. But when it was pointed out like this, I realised that I had been wrong. Thereupon I rose again and said; "I really went to the hot springs. It was wrong and I apologize." Then all again laughed. Whatever I say, they laugh. What a lot of boobs! See if you fellows can make a clean breast of your own fault like this! You fellows laugh because you can't talk straight.

After that the principal said that since it appeared that there will be no more opinions, he will consider the matter well and administer what he may deem a proper punishment. I may here add the result of the meeting. The students in the dormitory were given one week's confinement, and in addition to that, apologized to me. If they had not apologized, I intended to resign and go straight home, but as it was, it finally resulted in a bigger and still worse affair, of which more later. The principal then at the meeting said something to the effect that the manners of the students should be directed rightly by the teachers' influence, and as the first step, no teacher should patronize, if possible, the shops where edibles and drinks were served, excepting, however, in case of a farewell party or such social gatherings. He said he would like no teacher to go singly to eating houses of the lower kind — for instance, noodle-house or dango shop .... And again all laughed. Clown looked at Porcupine, said "tempura" and winked his eyes, but Porcupine regarded him in silence. Good!

My "think box" is not of superior quality, so things said by Badger were not clear to me, but I thought if a fellow can't hold the job of teacher in a middle school because he patronizes a noodle-house or dango shop, the fellow with bear-like appetite like me will never be able to hold it. If it was the case, they ought to have specified when calling for a teacher: one who does not eat noodle and dango. To give an appointment without reference to the matter at first, and then to proclaim that noodle or dango should not be eaten was a blow to a fellow like me who has no other petty hobby. Then Red Shirt again opened his mouth.

"Teachers of the middle school belong to the upper class of society and they should not be looking after material pleasures only, for it would eventually have effect upon their personal character. But we are human, and it would be intolerable in a small town like this to live without any means of affording some pleasure to ourselves, such as fishing, reading literary products, composing new style poems, or haiku (17-syllable poem). We should seek mental consolation of a higher order."

There seemed no prospect that he would quit the hot air. If it was a mental consolation to fish fertilisers on the sea, have goruki for Russian literature, or to pose a favorite geisha beneath pine tree, it would be quite as much a mental consolation to eat tempura noodle and swallow dango. Instead of dwelling on such sham consolations, he would find his time better spent by washing his red shirts. I became so exasperated that I asked; "Is it also a mental consolation to meet the Madonna?" No one laughed this time and looked at each other with queer faces, and Red Shirt himself hung his head, apparently embarrassed. Look at that! A good shot, eh? Only I was sorry for Hubbard Squash who, having heard the remark, became still paler.

CHAPTER VII.

THAT very night I left the boarding house. While I was packing up, the boss came to me and asked if there was anything wrong in the way I was treated. He said he would be pleased to correct it and suit me if I was sore at anything. This beats me, sure. How is it possible for so many boneheads to be in this world! I could not tell whether they wanted me to stay or get out. They're crazy. It would be disgrace for a Yedo kid to fuss about with such a fellow; so I hired a rikisha-man and speedily left the house.

I got out of the house all right, but had no place to go. The rikishaman asked me where I was going. I told him to follow me with his mouth shut, then he shall see and I kept on walking. I thought of going to Yamashiro-ya to avoid the trouble of hunting up a new boarding house, but as I had no prospect of being able to stay there long, I would have to renew the hunt sooner or later, so I gave up the idea. If I continued walking this way, I thought I might strike a house with the sign of "boarders taken" or something similar, and I would consider the first house with the sign the one provided for me by Heaven. I kept on going round and round through the quiet, decent part of the town when I found myself at Kajimachi. This used to be former samurai quarters where one had the least chance of finding any boarding house, and I was going to retreat to a more lively part of the town when a good idea occurred to me. Hubbard Squash whom I respected lived in this part of the town. He is a native of the town, and has lived in the house inherited from his great grandfather. He must be, I thought, well informed about nearly everything in this town. If I call on him for his help, he will perhaps find me a good boarding house. Fortunately, I called at his house once before, and there was no trouble in finding it out. I knocked at the door of a house, which I knew must be his, and a woman about fifty years old with an old fashioned paper-lantern in hand, appeared at the door. I do not despise young women, but when I see an aged woman, I feel much more solicitous. This is probably because I am so fond of Kiyo. This aged lady, who looked well-refined, was certainly mother of Hubbard Squash whom she resembled. She invited me inside, but I asked her to call him out for me. When he came I told him all the circumstances, and asked him if he knew any who would take me for a boarder. Hubbard Squash thought for a moment in a sympathetic mood, then said there was an old couple called Hagino, living in the rear of the street, who had asked him sometime ago to get some boarders for them as there are only two in the house and they had some vacant rooms. Hubbard Squash was kind enough to go along with me and find out if the rooms were vacant. They were.

From that night I boarded at the house of the Haginos. What surprised me was that on the day after I left the house of Ikagin, Clown stepped in and took the room I had been occupying. Well used to all sorts of tricks and crooks as I might have been, this audacity fairly knocked me off my feet. It was sickening.

I saw that I would be an easy mark for such people unless I brace up and try to come up, or down, to their level. It would be a high time indeed for me to be alive if it were settled that I would not get three meals a day without living on the spoils of pickpockets. Nevertheless, to hang myself, — healthy and vigorous as I am, — would be not only inexcusable before my ancestors but a disgrace before the public. Now I think it over, it would have been better for me to have started something like a milk delivery route with that six hundred yen as capital, instead of learning such a useless stunt as mathematics at the School of Physics. If I had done so, Kiyo could have stayed with me, and I could have lived without worrying about her so far a distance away. While I was with her I did not notice it, but separated thus I appreciated Kiyo as a good-natured old woman. One could not find a noble natured woman like Kiyo everywhere. She was suffering from a slight cold when I left Tokyo and I wondered how she was getting on now? Kiyo must have been pleased when she received the letter from me the other day. By the way, I thought it was time I was in receipt of the answer from her. I spent two or three days with things like this in my mind. I was anxious about the answer, and asked the old lady of the house if any letter came from Tokyo for me, and each time she would appear sympathetic and say no. The couple here, being formerly of samurai class, unlike the Ikagin couple, were both refined. The old man's recital of "utai" in a queer voice at night was somewhat telling on my nerves, but it was much easier on me as he did not frequent my room like Ikagin with the remark of "let me serve you tea."

The old lady once in a while would come to my room and chat on many things. She questioned me why I had not brought my wife with me. I asked her if I looked like one married, reminding her that I was only twenty four yet. Saying "it is proper for one to get married at twenty four" as a beginning, she recited that Mr. Blank married when he was twenty, that Mr. So-and-So has already two children at twenty two, and marshalled altogether about half a dozen examples, — quite a damper on my youthful theory. I will then get marred at twenty four, I said, and requested her to find me a good wife, and she asked me if I really meant it.

"Really? You bet! I can't help wanting to get married."

"I should suppose so. Everybody is just like that when young." This remark was a knocker; I could not say anything to that.

"But I'm sure you have a Madam already. I have seen to that with my own eyes."

"Well, they are sharp eyes. How have you seen it?"

"How? Aren't you often worried to death, asking if there's no letter from Tokyo?"

"By Jupiter! This beats me!"

"Hit the mark, haven't I?"

"Well, you probably have."

"But the girls of these days are different from what they used to be and you need a sharp look-out on them. So you'd better be careful."

"Do you mean that my Madam in Tokyo is behaving badly?"

"No, your Madam is all right."

"That makes me feel safe. Then about what shall I be careful?"

"Yours is all right. Though yours is all right ...."

"Where is one not all right?"

"Rather many right in this town. You know the daughter of the Toyamas?

"No, I do not."

"You don't know her yet? She is the most beautiful girl about here. She is so beautiful that the teachers in the school call her Madonna. You haven't heard that?"

"Ah, the Madonna! I thought it was the name of a geisha."

"No, Sir. Madonna is a foreign word and means a beautiful girl, doesn't it?"

"That may be. I'm surprised."

"Probably the name was given by the teacher of drawing."

"Was it the work of Clown?"

"No, it was given by Professor Yoshikawa."

"Is that Madonna not all right?"

"That Madonna-san is a Madonna not all right."

"What a bore! We haven't any decent woman among those with nicknames from old days. I should suppose the Madonna is not all right."

"Exactly. We have had awful women such as O-Matsu the Devil or Ohyaku the Dakki."

"Does the Madonna belong to that ring?"

"That Madonna-san, you know, was engaged to Professor Koga, — who brought you here, — yes, was promised to him."

"Ha, how strange! I never knew our friend Hubbard Squash was a fellow of such gallantry. We can't judge a man by his appearance. I'll be a bit more careful."

"The father of Professor Koga died last year, — up

to that time they had money and shares in a bank and were well off, — but since then things have grown worse, I don't know why. Professor Koga was too good-natured, in short, and was cheated, I presume. The wedding was delayed by one thing or another and there appeared the head teacher who fell in love with the Madonna head over heels and wanted to marry her."

"Red Shirt? He ought be hanged. I thought that shirt was not an ordinary kind of shirt. Well?"

"The head teacher proposed marriage through a go-between, but the Toyamas could not give a definite answer at once on account of their relations with the Kogas. They replied that they would consider the matter or something like that. Then Red Shirt-san worked up some ways and started visiting the Toyamas and has finally won the heart of the Miss. Red Shirt-san is bad, but so is Miss Toyama; they all talk bad of them. She had agreed to be married to Professor Koga and changed her mind because a Bachelor of Arts began courting her, — why, that would be an offense to the God of To-day."

"Of course. Not only of To-day but also of tomorrow and the day after; in fact, of time without end."

"So Hotta-san a friend of Koga-san, felt sorry for him and went to the head teacher to remonstrate with him. But Red Shirt-san said that he had no intention of taking away anybody who is promised to another. He may get married if the engagement is broken, he said, but at present he was only being acquainted with the Toyamas and he saw nothing wrong in his visiting the Toyamas. Hotta-san couldn't do anything and returned. Since then they say Red Shirt-san and Hotta-san are on bad terms."

"You do know many things, I should say. How did you get such details? I'm much impressed."

"The town is so small that I can know everything."

Yes, everything seems to be known more than one cares. Judging by her way, this woman probably knows about my tempura and dango affairs. Here was a pot that would make peas rattle! The meaning of the Madonna, the relations between Porcupine and Red Shirt became clear and helped me a deal. Only what puzzled me was the uncertainty as to which of the two was wrong. A fellow simple hearted like me could not tell which side he should help unless the matter was presented in black and white.

"Of Red Shirt and Porcupine, which is a better fellow?"

"What is Porcupine, Sir?"

"Porcupine means Hotta."

"Well, Hotta-san is physically strong, as strength goes, but Red Shirt-san is a Bachelor of Arts and has more ability. And Red Shirt-san is more gentle, as gentleness goes, but Hotta-san is more popular among the students."

"After all, which is better?"

"After all, the one who gets a bigger salary is greater, I suppose?"

There was no use of going on further in this way, and I closed the talk.

Two or three days after this, when I returned from the school, the old lady with a beaming smile, brought me a letter, saying, "Here you are Sir, at last. Take your time and enjoy it." I took it up and found it was from Kiyo. On the letter were two or three retransmission slips, and by these I saw the letter was sent from Yamashiro-ya to the Ikagins, then to the Haginos. Besides, it stayed at Yamashiro-ya for about one week; even letters seemed to stop in a hotel. I opened it, and it was a very long letter.

"When I received the letter from my Master Darling, I intended to write an answer at once. But I caught cold and was sick abed for about one week and the answer was delayed for which I beg your pardon. I am not well-used to writing or reading like girls in these days, and it required some efforts to get done even so poorly written a letter as this. I was going to ask my nephew to write it for me, but thought it inexcusable to my Master Darling when I should take special pains for myself. So I made a rough copy once, and then a clean copy. I finished the clean copy, in two days, but the rough copy took me four days. It may be difficult for you to read, but as I have written this letter with all my might, please read it to the end."

This was the introductory part of the letter in which, about four feet long, were written a hundred and one things. Well, it was difficult to read. Not only was it poorly written but it was a sort of juxtaposition of simple syllables that racked one's brain to make it clear where it stopped or where it began. I am quick-tempered and would refuse to read such a long, unintelligible letter for five yen, but I read this seriously from the first to the last. It is a fact that I read it through. My efforts were mostly spent in untangling letters and sentences; so I started reading it over again. The room had become a little dark, and this rendered it harder to read it; so finally I stepped out to the porch where I sat down and went over it carefully. The early autumn breeze wafted through the leaves of the banana trees, bathed me with cool evening air, rustled the letter I was holding and would have blown it clear to the hedge if I let it go. I did not mind anything like this, but kept on reading.

"Master Darling is simple and straight like a split bamboo by disposition," it says, "only too explosive. That's what worries me. If you brand other people with nicknames you will only make enemies of them; so don't use them carelessly; if you coin new ones, just tell them only to Kiyo in your letters. The country folk are said to be bad, and I wish you to be careful not have them do you. The weather must be worse than in Tokyo, and you should take care not to catch cold. Your letter is too short that I can't tell how things are going on with you. Next time write me a letter at least half the length of this one. Tipping the hotel with five yen is all right, but were you not short of money afterward? Money is the only thing one can depend upon when in the country and you should economize and be prepared for rainy days. I'm sending you ten yen by postal money order. I have that fifty yen my Master Darling gave me deposited in the Postal Savings to help you start housekeeping when you return to Tokyo, and taking out this ten, I have still forty yen left,—quite safe."

I should say women are very particular on many things.

When I was meditating with the letter flapping in my hand on the porch, the old lady opened the sliding partition and brought in my supper.

"Still poring over the letter? Must be a very long one, I imagine," she said.

"Yes, this is an important letter, so I'm reading it with the wind blowing it about," I replied — the reply which was nonsense even for myself, — and I sat down for supper. I looked in the dish on the tray, and saw the same old sweet potatoes again to-night. This new boarding house was more polite and considerate and refined than the Ikagins, but the grub was too poor stuff and that was one drawback. It was sweet potato yesterday, so it was the day before yesterday, and here it is again to-night. True, I declared myself very fond of sweet potatoes, but if I am fed with sweet potatoes with such insistency, I may soon have to quit this dear old world. I can't be laughing at Hubbard Squash; I shall become Sweet Potato myself before long. If it were Kiyo she would surely serve me with my favorite sliced tunny or fried kamaboko, but nothing doing with a tight, poor samurai. It seems best that I live with Kiyo. If I have to stay long in the school, I believe I would call her from Tokyo. Don't eat tempura, don't eat dango, and then get turned yellow by feeding on sweet potatoes only, in the boarding house. That's for an educator, and his place is really a hard one. I think even the priests of the Zen sect are enjoying better feed. I cleaned up the sweet potatoes, then took out two raw eggs from the drawer of my desk, broke them on the edge of the rice bowl, to tide it over. I have to get nourishment by eating raw eggs or something, or how can I stand the teaching of twenty one hours a week?

I was late for my bath to-day on account of the letter from Kiyo. But I would not like to drop off a single day since I had been there everyday. I thought I would take a train to-day, and coming to the station with the same old red towel dangling out of my hand, I found the train had just left two or three minutes ago, and had to wait for some time. While I was smoking a cigarette on a bench, my friend Hubbard Squash happened to come in. Since I heard the story about him from the old lady my sympathy for him had become far greater than ever. His reserve always appeared to me pathetic. It was no longer a case of merely pathetic; more than that. I was wishing to get his salary doubled, if possible, and have him marry Miss Toyama and send them to Tokyo for about one month on a pleasure trip. Seeing him, therefore, I motioned him to a seat beside me, addressing him cheerfully:

"Helloo, going to bath? Come and sit down here."

Hubbard Squash, appearing much awe-struck, said; "Don't mind me, Sir," and whether out of polite reluctance or I don't know what, remained standing.

"You have to wait for a little while before the next train starts; sit down; you'll be tired," I persuaded him again. In fact, I was so sympathetic for him that I wished to have him sit down by me somehow. Then with a "Thank you, Sir," he at last sat down. A fellow like Clown, always fresh, butts in where he is not wanted; or like Porcupine swaggers about with a face which says "Japan would be hard up without me," or like Red Shirt, self-satisfied in the belief of being the wholesaler of gallantry and of cosmetics. Or like Badger who appears to say; "If 'Education' were alive and put on a frockcoat, it would look like me." One and all in one way or other have bravado, but I have never seen any one like this Hubbard Squash, so quiet and resigned, like a doll taken for a ransom. His face is rather swollen but for the Madonna to cast off such a splendid fellow and give preference to Red Shirt, was frivolous beyond my understanding. Put how many dozens of Red Shirt you like together, it will not make one husband of stuff to beat Hubbard Squash.

"Is anything wrong with you? You look quite fatigued," I asked.

"No, I have no particular ailments ...."

"That's good. Poor health is the worst thing one can get."

"You appear very strong."

"Yes, I'm thin, but never got sick. That's something I don't like."

Hubbard Squash smiled at my words. Just then I heard some young girlish laughs at the entrance, and incidentally looking that way, I saw a "peach." A beautiful girl, tall, white-skinned, with her head done up in "high-collared" style, was standing with a woman of about forty-five or six, in front of the ticket window. I am not a fellow given to describing a belle, but there was no need to repeat asserting that she was beautiful. I felt as if I had warmed a crystal ball with perfume and held it in my hand. The older woman was shorter, but as she resembled the younger, they might be mother and daughter. The moment I saw them, I forgot all about Hubbard Squash, and was intently gazing at the young beauty. Then I was a bit startled to see Hubbard Squash suddenly get up and start walking slowly toward them. I wondered if she was not the Madonna. The three were courtesying in front of the ticket window, some distance away from me, and I could not hear what they were talking about.

The clock at the station showed the next train to start in five minutes. Having lost my partner, I became impatient and longed for the train to start as soon as possible, when a fellow rushed into the station excited. It was Red Shirt. He had on some fluffy clothes, loosely tied round with a silk-crepe girdle, and wound to it the same old gold chain. That gold chain is stuffed. Red Shirt thinks nobody knows it and is making a big show of it, but I have been wise. Red Shirt stopped short, stared around, and then after bowing politely to the three still in front of the ticket window, made a remark or two, and hastily turned toward me. He came up to me, walking in his usual cat's style, and hallooed.

"You too going to bath? I was afraid of missing the train and hurried up, but we have three or four minutes yet. Wonder if that clock is right?"

He took out his gold watch, and remarking it wrong about two minutes sat down beside me. He never turned toward the belle, but with his chin on the top of a cane, steadily looked straight before him. The older woman would occasionally glance toward Red Shirt, but the younger kept her profile away. Surely she was the Madonna.

The train now arrived with a shrill whistle and the passengers hastened to board. Red Shirt jumped into the first class coach ahead of all. One cannot brag much about boarding the first class coach here. It cost only five sen for the first and three sen for the second to Sumida; even I paid for the first and a white ticket. The country fellows, however, being all close, seemed to regard the expenditure of the extra two sen a serious matter and mostly boarded the second class. Following Red Shirt, the Madonna and her mother entered the first class. Hubbard Squash regularly rides in the second class. He stood at the door of a second class coach and appeared somewhat hesitating, but seeing me coming, took decisive steps and jumped into the second. I felt sorry for him — I do not know why — and followed him into the same coach. Nothing wrong in riding on the second with a ticket for the first, I believe.

At the hot springs, going down from the third floor to the bath room in bathing gown, again I met Hubbard Squash. I feel my throat clogged up and unable to speak at a formal gathering, but otherwise I am rather talkative; so I opened conversation with him. He was so pathetic and my compassion was aroused to such an extent that I considered it the duty of a Yedo kid to console him to the best of my ability. But Hubbard Squash was not responsive. Whatever I said, he would only answer "eh?" or "umh," and even these with evident effort. Finally I gave up my sympathetic attempt and cut off the conversation.

I did not meet Red Shirt at the bath. There are many bath rooms, and one does not necessarily meet the fellows at the same bath room though he might come on the same train. I thought it nothing strange. When I got out of the bath, I found the night bright with the moon. On both sides of the street stood willow trees which cast their shadows on the road. I would take a little stroll, I thought. Coming up toward north, to the end of the town, one sees a large gate to the left. Opposite the gate stands a temple and both sides of the approach to the temple are lined with houses with red curtains. A tenderloin inside a temple gate is an unheard-of phenomenon. I wanted to go in and have a look at the place, but for fear I might get another kick from Badger, I passed it by. A flat house with narrow lattice windows and black curtain at the entrance, near the gate, is the place where I ate dango and committed the blunder. A round lantern with the signs of sweet meats hung outside and its light fell on the trunk of a willow tree close by. I hungered to have a bite of dango, but went away forbearing.

To be unable to eat dango one is so fond of eating, is tragic. But to have one's betrothed change her love to another, would be more tragic. When I think of Hubbard Squash, I believe that I should not complain if I cannot eat dango or anything else for three days. Really there is nothing so unreliable a creature as man. As far as her face goes, she appears the least likely to commit so stony-hearted an act as this. But the beautiful person is cold-blooded and Koga-san who is swollen like a pumpkin soaked in water, is a gentleman to the core, — that's where we have to be on the look-out. Porcupine whom I had thought candid was said to have incited the students and he whom then I regarded an agitator, demanded of the principal a summary punishment of the students. The disgustingly snobbish Red Shirt is unexpectedly considerate and warns me in ways more than one, but then he won the Madonna by crooked means. He denies, however, having schemed anything crooked about the Madonna, and says he does not care to marry her unless her engagement with Koga is broken. When Ikagin beat me out of his house, Clown enters and takes my room. Viewed from any angle, man is unreliable. If I write these things to Kiyo, it would surprise her. She would perhaps say that because it is the west side of Hakone that the town had all the freaks and crooks dumped in together.*

I do not by nature worry about little things, and had come so far without minding anything. But hardly a month had passed since I came here, and I have begun to regard the world quite uneasily. I have not met with any particularly serious affairs, but I feel as if I had grown five or six years older. Better say "good by" to this old spot soon and return to Tokyo, I thought. While strolling thus thinking on various matters, I had passed the stone bridge and come up to the levee of the Nozeri river. The word river sounds too big; it is a shallow stream of about six feet wide. If one goes on along the levee for about twelve blocks, he reaches the Aioi village where there is a temple of Kwanon.

Looking back at the town of the hot springs, I see red lights gleaming amid the pale moon beams. Where the sound of the drum is heard must be the tenderloin. The stream is shallow but fast, whispering incessantly. When I had covered about three blocks walking leisurely upon the bank, I perceived a shadow ahead. Through the light of the moon, I found there were two shadows. They were probably

---

* An old saying goes that east of the Hakone pass, there are no apparitions or freaks.

village youngsters returning from the hot springs, though they did not sing, and were exceptionally quiet for that.

I kept on walking, and I was faster than they. The two shadows became larger. One appeared like a woman. When I neared them within about sixty feet, the man, on hearing my footsteps, turned back. The moon was shining from behind me. I could see the manner of the man then and something queer struck me. They resumed their walk as before. And I chased them on at full speed. The other party, unconscious, walked slowly. I could now hear their voices distinctly. The levy was about six feet wide, and would allow only three abreast. I easily passed them, and turning back gazed squarely into the face of the man. The moon generously bathed my face with its beaming light. The fellow uttered a low "ah," and suddenly turning sideway, said to the woman "Let's go back." They traced their way back toward the hot springs town.

Was it the intention of Red Shirt to hush the matter up by pretending ignorance, or was it lack of nerve? I was not the only fellow who suffered the consequence of living in a small narrow town.

CHAPTER VIII.

O N my way back from the fishing to which I was invited by Red Shirt, and since then, I began to suspect Porcupine. When the latter wanted me to get out of Ikagin's house on sham pretexts, I regarded him a decidedly unpleasant fellow. But as Porcupine, at the teachers' meeting, contrary to my expectation, stood firmly for punishing the students to the fullest extent of the school regulations, I thought it queer. When I heard from the old lady about Porcupine volunteering himself for the sake of Hubbard Squash to stop Red Shirt meddling with the Madonna, I clapped my hands and hoorayed for him. Judging by these facts, I began to wonder if the wrong-doer might be not Porcupine, but Red Shirt the crooked one. He instilled into my head some flimsy hearsay plausibly and in a round-about-way. At this juncture I saw Red Shirt taking a walk with the Madonna on the levee of the Nozeri river, and I decided that Red Shirt may be a scoundrel. I am not sure of his being really a scoundrel at heart, but at any rate he is not a good fellow. He is a fellow with a double face. A man deserves no confidence unless he is as straight as the bamboo. One may fight a straight fellow, and feel satisfied. We cannot lose sight of the fact that Red Shirt or his kind who is kind, gentle, refined, and takes pride in his pipe had to be looked sharp, for I could not be too careful in getting into a scrap with a fellow of this type. I may fight, but I would not get square games like the wrestling matches at the Wrestling Amphitheatre in Tokyo. Come to think of it, Porcupine who turned against me and startled the whole teachers' room over the amount of one sen and a half is far more like a man. When he stared at me with owlish eyes at the teachers' meeting, I branded him as a spiteful guy, but as I consider the matter now, he is better than the feline voice of Red Shirt. To tell the truth, I tried to get reconciled with Porcupine, and after the meeting, spoke a word or two to him, but he shut up like a clam and kept glaring at me. So I became sore, and let it go at that.

Porcupine has not spoken to me since. The one sen and a half which I paid him back upon the desk, is still there, well covered with dust. I could not touch it, nor would Porcupine take it. This one sen and a half has become a barrier between us two. We two were cursed with this one sen and a half. Later indeed I got sick of its sight that I hated to see it.

While Porcupine and I were thus estranged, Red Shirt and I continued friendly relations and associated together. On the day following my accidental meeting with him near the Nozeri river, for instance, Red Shirt came to my desk as soon as he came to the school, and asked me how I liked the new boarding house. He said we would go together for fishing Russian literature again, and talked on many things. I felt a bit piqued, and said, "I saw you twice last night," and he answered, "Yes, at the station. Do you go there at that time every day? Isn't it late?" I startled him with the remark; "I met you on the levee of the Nozeri river too, didn't I?" and he replied, "No, I didn't go in that direction. I returned right after my bath."

What is the use of trying to keep it dark. Didn't we meet actually face to face? He tells too many lies.

If one can hold the job of a head teacher and act in this fashion, I should be able to run the position of Chancellor of a university. From this time on, my confidence in Red Shirt became still less. I talk with Red Shirt whom I do not trust, and I keep silent with Porcupine whom I respect. Funny things do happen in this world.

One day Red Shirt asked me to come over to his house as he had something to tell me, and much as I missed the trip to the hot springs, I started for his house at about 4 o'clock. Red Shirt is single, but in keeping with the dignity of a head teacher, he gave up the boarding house life long ago, and lives in a fine house. The house rent, I understood, was nine yen and fifty sen. The front entrance was so attractive that I thought if one can live in such a splendid house at nine yen and a half in the country, it would be a good game to call Kiyo from Tokyo and make her heart glad. The younger brother of Red Shirt answered my bell. This brother gets his lessons on algebra and mathematics from me at the school. He stands no show in his school work, and being a "migratory bird" is more wicked than the native boys.

I met Red Shirt. Smoking the same old unsavory amber pipe, he said something to the following effect:

"Since you've been with us, our work has been more satisfactory than it was under your predecessor, and the principal is very glad to have got the right person in the right place. I wish you to work as hard as you can, for the school is depending upon you."

"Well, is that so. I don't think I can work any harder than now ...."

"What you're doing now is enough. Only don't forget what I told you the other day."

"Meaning that one who helps me find a boarding house is dangerous?"

"If you state it so baldly, there is no meaning to it .... But that's all right, ... I believe you understand the spirit of my advice. And if you keep on in the way you're going to-day ...... We have not been blind ...... we might offer you a better treatment later on if we can manage it."

"In salary? I don't care about the salary, though the more the better."

"And fortunately there is going to be one teacher transferred, ... however, I can't guarantee, of course, until I talk it over with the principal ...... and we might give you something out of his salary."

"Thank you. Who is going to be transferred?"

"I think I may tell you now; 'tis going to be Announced soon. Koga is the man."

"But isn't Koga-san a native of this town?"

"Yes, he is. But there are some circumstances ...... and it is partly by his own preference."

"Where is he going?"

"To Nobeoka in Hiuga province. As the place is so far away, he is going there with his salary raised a grade higher."

"Is some one coming to take his place?"

"His successor is almost decided upon."

"Well, that's fine, though I'm not very anxious to have my salary raised."

"I'm going to talk to the principal about that anyway. And, we may have to ask you to work more some time later ...... and the principal appears to be of the same opinion .... I want you to go ahead with that in your mind."

"Going to increase my working hours?"

"No. The working hours may be reduced ......"

"The working hours shortened and yet work more? Sounds funny."

"It does sound funny ...... I can't say definitely just yet ...... it means that we way have to ask you to assume more responsibility."

I could not make out what he meant. To assume more responsibility might mean my appointment to the senior instructor of mathematics, but Porcupine is the senior instructor and there is no danger of his resigning. Besides, he is so very popular among the students that his transfer or discharge would be inadvisable. Red Shirt always misses the point. And though he did not get to the point, the object of my visit was ended. We talked a while on sundry matters, Red Shirt proposing a farewell dinner party for Hubbard Squash, asking me if I drink liquor and praising Hubbard Squash as an amiable gentleman, etc. Finally he changed the topic and asked me if I take an interest in "haiku"* Here is where I beat it, I thought, and, saying "No, I don't, good by," hastily left the house. The "haiku" should be a diversion of Baseo† or the boss of a barber-shop. It would not do for the teacher of mathematics to rave over the old wooden bucket and the morning glory.‡

---

* The 17-syllable poem.

† A famous composer of the poem.

‡ There is a well-known 17-syllable poem describing the scene of morning glories entwining around the wooden bucket.

I returned home and thought it over. Here is a man whose mental process defies a layman's understanding. He is going to court hardships in a strange part of the country in preference of his home and the school where he is working, — both of which should satisfy most anybody, — because he is tired of them. That may be all right if the strange place happens to be a lively metropolis where electric cars run, — but of all places, why Nobeoka in Hiuga province? This town here has a good steamship connection, yet I became sick of it and longed for home before one month had passed. Nobeoka is situated in the heart of a most mountainous country. According to Red Shirt, one has to make an all-day ride in a wagonette to Miyazaki, after he had left the vessel, and from Miyazaki another all-day ride in a rikisha to Nobeoka. Its name alone does not commend itself as civilized. It sounds like a town inhabited by men and monkeys in equal numbers. However sage-like Hubbard Squash might be I thought he would not become a friend of monkeys of his own choice. What a curious slant!

Just then the old lady brought in my supper. "Sweet potatoes again?" I asked, and she said, "No, Sir, it is tofu to-night." They are about the same thing.

"Say, I understand Koga-san is going to Nobeoka."

"Isn't it too bad?"

"Too bad? But it can't be helped if he goes there by his own preference."

"Going there by his own preference? Who, Sir?"

"Who? Why, he! Isn't Professor Koga going there by his own choice?"

"That's wrong Mr. Wright, Sir."

"Ha, Mr. Wright, is it? But Red Shirt told me so just now. If that's wrong Mr. Wright, then Red Shirt is blustering Mr. Bluff."

"What the head-teacher says is believable, but so Koga-san does not wish to go."

Our old lady is impartial, and that is good. "Well, what's the matter?"

"The mother of Koga-san was here this morning, and told me all the circumstances."

"Told you what circumstances?"

"Since the father of Koga-san died, they have not been quite as well off as we might have supposed, and the mother asked the principal if his salary could not be raised a little as Koga-san has been in service for four years. See?"

"Well?"

"The principal said that he would consider the matter, and she felt satisfied and expected the announcement of the increase before long. She hoped for its coming this month or next. Then the principal called Koga-san to his office one day and said that he was sorry but the school was short of money and could not raise his salary. But he said there is an opening in Nobeoka which would give him five yen extra a month and he thought that would suit his purpose, and the principal had made all arrangements and told Koga-san he had better go ...."

"That wasn't a friendly talk but a command. Wasn't it?"

"Yes, Sir. Koga-san told the principal that he liked to stay here better at the old salary than go elsewhere on an increased salary, because he has his own house and is living with his mother. But the matter has all been settled, and his successor already appointed and it couldn't be helped, said the principal."

"Hum, that's a jolly good trick, I should say. Then Koga-san has no liking to go there? No wonder I thought it strange. We would have to go a long way to find any blockhead to do a job in such a mountain village and get acquainted with monkeys for five yen extra."

"What is a blockhead, Sir?"

"Well, let go at that. It was all the scheme of Red Shirt. Deucedly underhand scheme, I declare. It was a stab from behind. And he means to raise my salary by that; that's not right. I wouldn't take that raise. Let's see if he can raise it."

"Is your salary going to be raised, Sir?"

"Yes, they said they would raise mine, but I'm thinking of refusing it."

"Why do you refuse?"

"Why or no why, it's going to be refused. Say, Red Shirt is a fool; he is a coward."

"He may be a coward, but if he raises your salary, it would be best for you to make no fuss, but accept it. One is apt to get grouchy when young, but will always repent when he is grown up and thinks that it was pity he hadn't been a little more patient. Take an old woman's advice for once, and if Red Shirt-san says he will raise your salary, just take it with thanks."

"It's no business of you old people."

The old lady withdrew in silence. The old man is heard singing "utai" in the off-key voice. "Utai," I think, is a stunt which purposely makes a whole show a hard nut to crack by giving to it difficult tunes, whereas one could better understand it by reading it. I cannot fathom what is in the mind of the old man who groans over it every night untired. But I'm not in a position to be fooling with "utai." Red Shirt said he would have my salary raised, and though I did not care much about it, I accepted it because there was no use of leaving the money lying around. But I cannot, for the love of Mike, be so inconsiderate as to skin the salary of a fellow teacher who is being transferred against his will. What in thunder do they mean by sending him away so far as Nobeoka when the fellow prefers to remain in his old position? Even Dazai-no-Gonnosutsu did not have to go farther than about Hakata; even Matagoro Kawai* stopped at Sagara. I shall not feel satisfied unless I see Red Shirt and tell him I refuse the raise.

I dressed again and went to his house. The same younger brother of Red Shirt again answered the bell, and looked at me with eyes which plainly said, "You here again?" I will come twice or thrice or as many times as I want to if there is business. I might rouse them out of their beds at midnight; — it is possible, who knows. Don't mistake me for one coming to coax the head teacher. I was here to give back my salary. The younger brother said that there is a visitor just now, and I told him the front door will do; won't take more than a minute, and he went in. Looking about my feet, I found a pair of thin, matted wooden clogs, and I heard some one in the house saying, "Now we're banzai." I noticed that the visitor

---

* The persons in exile, well-known in Japanese history.

was Clown. Nobody but Clown could make such a squeaking voice and wear such clogs as are worn by cheap actors.

After a while Red Shirt appeared at the door with a lamp in his hand, and said, "Come in; it's no other than Mr. Yoshikawa."

"This is good enough," I said, "it won't take long." I looked at his face which was the color of a boiled lobster. He seemed to have been drinking with Clown.

"You told me that you would raise my salary, but I've changed my mind, and have come here to decline the offer."

Red Shirt, thrusting out the lamp forward, and intently staring at me, was unable to answer at the moment. He appeared blank. Did he think it strange that here was one fellow, only one in the world, who does not want his salary raised; or was he taken aback that I should come back so soon even if I wished to decline it; or was it both combined, he stood there silent with his mouth in a queer shape.

"I accepted your offer because I understood that Mr. Koga was being transferred by his own preference ...."

"Mr. Koga is really going to be transferred by his own preference."

"No, Sir. He would like to stay here. He doesn't mind his present salary if he can stay."

"Have you heard it from Mr. Koga himself?"

"No, not from him."

"Then, from who?"

"The old lady in my boarding house told me what she heard from the mother of Mr. Koga."

"Then the old woman in your boarding house told you so?"

"Well, that's about the size of it."

"Excuse me, but I think you are wrong. According to what you say, it seems as if you would believe what the old woman in the boarding house tells you, but would not believe what your head teacher tells you. Am I right to understand it that way?"

I was stuck. A Bachelor of Arts is confoundedly good in oratorical combat. He gets hold of an unexpected point, and pushes the other backward. My father used to tell me that I am too careless and no good, and now indeed I look that way. I ran out of the house on the moment's impulse when I heard the story from the old lady, and in fact I had not heard the story from either Hubbard Squash or his mother. In consequence, when I was challenged in this Bachelor-of-Arts fashion, it was a bit difficult to defend myself.

I could not defend his frontal attack, but I had already declared in my mind a lack of confidence on Red Shirt. The old lady in the boarding house may be tight and a grabber, I do not doubt it, but she is a woman who tells no lie. She is not double faced like Red Shirt, I was helpless, so I answered.

"What you say might be right, — anyway, I decline the raise."

"That's still funnier. I thought your coming here now was because you had found a certain reason for which you could not accept the raise. Then it is hard to understand to see you still insisting on declining the raise in spite of the reason having been eradicated by my explanation."

"It may be hard to understand, but anyway I don't want it."

"If you don't like it so much, I wouldn't force it on you. But if you change your mind within two or three hours with no particular reason, it would affect your credit in future."

"I don't care if it does affect it."

"That can't be. Nothing is more important than credit for us. Supposing, the boss of the boarding house ...."

"Not the boss, but the old lady."

"Makes no difference, — suppose what the old woman in the boarding house told you was true, the raise of your salary is not to be had by reducing the income of Mr. Koga, is it? Mr. Koga is going to Nobeoka; his successor is coming. He comes on a salary a little less than that of Mr. Koga, and we propose to add the surplus money to your salary, and you need not be shy. Mr. Koga will be promoted; the successor is to start on less pay, and if you could be raised, I think everything is satisfactory to all concerned. If you don't like it, that's all right, but suppose you think it over once more at home?"

My brain is not of the best stuff, and if another fellow flourishes his eloquence like this, I usually think, "Well, perhaps I was wrong," and consider myself defeated, but not so to-night. From the time I came to this town I felt prejudiced against Red Shirt. Once I had thought of him in a different light, taking him for a fellow kind-hearted and feminised. His kindness, however, began to look like anything but kindness, and as a result, I have been getting sick of him. So no matter how he might glory himself in logical grandiloquence, or how he might attempt to out-talk me in a head-teacher-style, I don't care a snap. One who shines in argument is not necessarily a good fellow, while the other who is out-talked is not necessarily a bad fellow, either. Red Shirt is very, very reasonable as far as his reasoning goes, but however graceful he may appear, he cannot win my respect. If money, authority or reasoning can command admiration, loan sharks, police officers or college professors should be liked best by all. I cannot be moved in the least by the logic of so insignificant a fellow as the head teacher of a middle school. Man works by preference, not by logic.

"What you say is right, but I have begun to dislike the raise, so I decline. It will be the same if I think it over. Good by." And I left the house of Red Shirt. The solitary Milky Way hung high in the sky.

CHAPTER IX.

When I went to the school, in the morning of the day the farewell dinner party was to be held, Porcupine suddenly spoke to me;

"The other day I asked you to quit the Ikagins because Ikagin begged of me to have you leave there as you were too tough, and I believed him. But I heard afterward that Ikagin is a crook and often passes imitation of famous drawings for originals. I think what he told me about you must be a lie. He tried to sell pictures and curios to you, but as you shook him off, he told some false stories on you. I did very wrong by you because I did not know his character, and wish you would forgive me." And he offered me a lengthy apology.

Without saying a word, I took up the one sen and a half which was lying on the desk of Porcupine, and put it into my purse. He asked me in a wondering tone, if I meant to take it back. I explained, "Yes. I didn't like to have you treat me and expected to pay this back at all hazard, but as I think about it, I would rather have you treated me after all; so I'm going to take it back."

Porcupine laughed heartily and asked me why I had not taken it back sooner. I told him that I wanted to more than once, in fact, but somehow felt shy and left it there. I was so sick of that one sen and a half these days that I shunned the sight of it when I came to the school, I said. He said "You're a deucedly unyielding sport," and I answered "You're obstinate." Then ensued the following give-and-take between us two;

"Where were you born anyway?"

"I'm a Yedo kid."

"Ah, a Yedo kid, eh? No wonder I thought you a pretty stiff neck."

"And you?"

"I'm from Aizu."

"Ha, Aizu guy, eh? You've got reason to be obstinate. Going to the farewell dinner to-day?"

"Sure. You?"

"Of course I am. I intend to go down to the beach to see Koga-san off when he leaves."

"The farewell dinner should be a big blow-out. You come and see. I'm going to get soused to the neck."

"You get loaded all you want. I quit the place right after I finish my plates. Only fools fight booze."

"You're a fellow who picks up a fight too easy. It shows up the characteristic of the Yedo kid well."

"I don't care. Say, before you go to the farewell dinner, come to see me. I want to tell you something."

Porcupine came to my room as promised. I had been in full sympathy with Hubbard Squash these days, and when it came to his farewell dinner, my pity for him welled up so much that I wished I could go to Nobeoka for him myself. I thought of making a parting address of burning eloquence at the dinner to grace the occasion, but my speech which rattles off like that of the excited spieler of New York would not become the place. I planned to take the breath out of Red Shirt by employing Porcupine who has a thunderous voice. Hence my invitation to him before we started for the party.

I commenced by explaining the Madonna affair, but Porcupine, needless to say, knew more about it than I. Telling about my meeting Red Shirt on the Nozeri river, I called him a fool. Porcupine then said; "You call everybody a fool. You called me a fool to-day at the school. If I'm a fool, Red Shirt isn't," and insisted that he was not in the same group with Red Shirt. "Then Red Shirt may be a four-flusher," I said and he approved this new alias with enthusiasm. Porcupine is physically strong, but when it comes to such terms, he knows less than I do. I guess all Aizu guys are about the same.

Then, when I disclosed to him about the raise of my salary and the advance hint on my promotion by Red Shirt, Porcupine pished, and said, "Then he means to discharge me." "Means to discharge you? But you mean to get discharged?" I asked. "Bet you, no. If I get fired, Red Shirt will have to go with me," he remarked with a lordly air. I insisted on knowing how he was going to get Red Shirt kicked out with him, and he answered that he had not thought so far yet. Yes, Porcupine looks strong, but seems to be possessed of no abundance of brain power. I told him about my refusal of the raise of my salary, and the Gov'nur was much pleased, praising me with the remark, "That's the stuff for Yedo kids."

"If Hubbard Squash does not like to go down to Nobeoka, why didn't you do something to enable him to remain here," I asked, and Porcupine said that when he heard the story from Hubbard Squash, everything had been settled already, but he had asked the principal twice and Red Shirt once to have the transfer order cancelled, but to no purpose. Porcupine bitterly condemned Hubbard Squash for being too good-natured. If Hubbard Squash, he said, had either flatly refused or delayed the answer on the pretext of considering it, when Red Shirt raised the question of transfer, it would have been better for him. But he was fooled by the oily tongue of Red Shirt, had accepted the transfer outright, and all efforts by Porcupine who was moved by the tearful appeal of the mother, proved unavailing.

I said; "The transfer of Koga is nothing but a trick of Red Shirt to cop the Madonna by sending Hubbard Squash away."

"Yes," said Porcupine "That must be. Red Shirt looks gentle, but plays nasty tricks. He is a sonova-gun for when some one finds fault with him, he has excuses prepared already. Nothing but a sound thumping will be effective for fellows like him."

He rolled up his sleeves over his plump arms as he spoke. I asked him, by the way, if he knew jiu-jitsu, because his arms looked powerful. Then he put force in his forearm, and told me to touch it. I felt its swelled muscle which was hard as the pumice stone in the public bathhouse.

I was deeply impressed by his massive strength, and asked him if he could not knock five or six of Red Shirt in a bunch. "Of course," he said, and as he extended and bent back the arm, the lumpy muscle rolled round and round, which was very amusing. According to the statement of Porcupine himself, this muscle, if he bends the arm back with force, would snap a paper-string wound around it twice. I said I might do the same thing if it were a paper-string, and he challenged me. "No, you can't," he said. "See if you can." As it would not look well if I failed, I did not try.

"Say, after you have drunk all you want to-night at the dinner, take a fall out of Red Shirt and Clown, eh?" I suggested to him for fun. Porcupine thought for a moment and said, "Not to-night, I guess." I wanted to know why, and he pointed out that it would be bad for Koga.

"Besides, if I'm going to give it to them at all, I've got to get them red handed in their dirty scheme, or all the blame will be on me," he added discretely. Even Porcupine seems to have wiser judgment than I.

"Then make a speech and praise Mr. Koga sky-high. My speech becomes sort of jumpy, wanting dignity. And at any formal gathering, I get lumpy in my throat, and can't speak. So I leave it to you," I said.

"That's a strange disease. Then you can't speak in the presence of other people? It would be awkward, I suppose," he said, and I told him not quite as awkward as he might think.

About then, the time for the farewell dinner party arrived, and I went to the hall with Porcupine. The dinner party was to be held at Kashin-tei which is said to be the leading restaurant in the town, but I had never been in the house before. This restaurant, I understood, was formerly the private residence of the chief retainer of the daimyo of the province, and its condition seemed to confirm the story. The residence of a chief retainer transformed into a restaurant was like making a saucepan out of warrior's armor.

When we two came there, about all of the guests were present. They formed two or three groups in the spacious room of fifty mats. The alcove in this room, in harmony with its magnificence, was very large. The alcove in the fifteen-mat room which I occupied at Yamashiro-ya made a small showing beside it. I measured it and found it was twelve feet wide. On the right, in the alcove, there was a seto-ware flower vase, painted with red designs, in which was a large branch of pine tree. Why the pine twigs, I did not know, except that they are in no danger of withering for many a month to come, and are economical. I asked the teacher of natural history where that seto-ware flower vase is made. He told me it was not a seto-ware but an imari. Isn't imari seto-ware? I wondered audibly, and the natural history man laughed. I heard afterward that we call it a seto-ware because it is made in Seto. I'm a Yedo kid, and thought all china was seto-wares. In the center of the alcove was hung a panel on which were written twenty eight letters, each letter as large as my face. It was poorly written; so poorly indeed that I enquired of the teacher of Confucius why would such a poor work be hung in apparent show of pride. He explained that it was written by Kaioku a famous artist in the writing, but Kaioku or anyone else, I still declare the work poorly done.

By and by, Kawamura, the clerk, requested all to be seated. I chose one in front of a pillar so I could lean against it. Badger sat in front of the panel of Kaioku in Japanese full dress. On his left sat Red Shirt similarly dressed, and on his right Hubbard Squash, as the guest of honor, in the same kind of dress. I was dressed in a European suit, and being unable to sit down, squatted on my legs at once. The teacher of physical culture next to me, though in the same kind of rags as mine, sat squarely in Japanese fashion. As a teacher of his line he appeared to have well trained himself. Then the dinner trays were served and the bottles placed beside them. The manager of the day stood up and made a brief opening address. He was followed by Badger and Red Shirt. These two made farewell addresses, and dwelt at length on Hubbard Squash being an ideal teacher and gentleman, expressing their regret, saying his departure was a great loss not only to the school but to them in person. They concluded that it could not be helped, however, since the transfer was due to his own earnest desire and for his own convenience. They appeared to be not in the least ashamed by telling such a lie at a farewell dinner. Particularly, Red Shirt, of these three, praised Hubbard Squash in lavish terms. He went so far as to declare that to lose this true friend was a great personal loss to him. Moreover, his tone was so impressive in its same old gentle tone that one who listens to him for the first time would be sure to be misled. Probably he won the Madonna by this same trick. While Red Shirt was uttering his farewell buncomb, Porcupine who sat on the other side across me, winked at me. As an answer of this, I "snooked" at him.

No sooner had Red Shirt sat down than Porcupine stood up, and highly rejoiced, I clapped hands. At this Badger and others glanced at me, and I felt that I blushed a little.

"Our principal and other gentlemen," he said, "particularly the head teacher, expressed their sincere regret at Mr. Koga's transfer. I am of a different opinion, and hope to see him leave the town at the earliest possible moment. Nobeoka is an out-of-the-way, backwoods town, and compared with this town, it may have more material inconveniences, but according to what I have heard, Nobeoka is said to be a town where the customs are simple and untainted, and the teachers and students still strong in the straightforward characteristics of old days. I am convinced that in Nobeoka there is not a single high-collared guy who passes round threadbare remarks, or who with smooth face, entraps innocent people. I am sure that a man like Mr. Koga, gentle and honest, will surely be received with an enthusiastic welcome there. I heartily welcome this transfer for the sake of Mr. Koga. In concluding, I hope that when he is settled down at Nobeoka, he will find a lady qualified to become his wife, and form a sweet home at an early date and incidentally let the inconstant, unchaste sassy old wench die ashamed ...... a'hum, a'hum!"

He coughed twice significantly and sat down. I thought of clapping my hands again, but as it would draw attention, I refrained. When Porcupine finished his speech, Hubbard Squash arose politely, slipped out of his seat, went to the furthest end of the room, and having bowed to all in a most respectful manner, acknowledged the compliments in the following way;

"On the occasion of my going to Kyushu for my personal convenience, I am deeply impressed and appreciate the way my friends have honored me with this magnificent dinner .... The farewell addresses by our principal and other gentlemen will be long held in my fondest recollection .... I am going far away now, but I hope my name is included in the future as in the past in the list of friends of the gentlemen here to-night."

Then again bowing, he returned to his seat. There was no telling how far the "good-naturedness" of Hubbard Squash might go. He had respectfully thanked the principal and the head teacher who had been fooling him. And it was not a formal, cut-and-dried reply he made, either; by his manner, tone and face, he appeared to have been really grateful from his heart. Badger and Red Shirt should have blushed when they were addressed so seriously by so good a man as Hubbard Squash, but they only listened with long faces.

After the exchange of addresses, a sizzling sound was heard here and there, and I too tried the soup which tasted like anything but soup. There was kamaboko in the kuchitori dish, but instead of being snow white as it should be, it looked grayish, and was more like a poorly cooked chikuwa. The sliced tunny was there, but not having been sliced fine, passed the throat like so many pieces of chopped raw tunny. Those around me, however, ate with ravenous appetite. They have not tasted, I guess, the real Yedo dinner.

Meanwhile the bottles began passing round, and all became more or less "jacked up." Clown proceeded to the front of the principal and submissively drank to his health. A beastly fellow, this! Hubbard Squash made a round of all the guests, drinking to their health. A very onerous job, indeed. When he came to me and proposed my health, I abandoned the squatting posture and sat up straight.

"Too bad to see you go away so soon. When are you going? I want to see you off at the beach," I said.

"Thank you, Sir. But never mind that. You're busy," he declined. He might decline, but I was determined to get excused for the day and give him a rousing send-off.

Within about an hour from this, the room became pretty lively.

"Hey, have another, hic; ain't goin', hic, have one on me?" One or two already in a pickled state appeared on the scene. I was little tired, and going out to the porch, was looking at the old fashioned garden by the dim star light, when Porcupine came.

"How did you like my speech? Wasn't it grand, though!" he remarked in a highly elated tone. I protested that while I approved 99 per cent, of his speech, there was one per cent, that I did not. "What's that one per cent?" he asked.

"Well, you said, ... there is not a single high-collared guy who with smooth face entraps innocent people ...."

"Yes."

"A 'high-collared guy' isn't enough."

"Then what should I say?"

"Better say, — 'a high-collared guy, swindler, bastard, super-swanker, doubleface, bluffer, totempole, spotter, who looks like a dog as he yelps.'"

"I can't get my tongue to move so fast. You're eloquent. In the first place, you know a great many simple words. Strange that you can't make a speech."

"I reserve these words for use when I chew the rag. If it comes to speech-making, they don't come out so smoothly."

"Is that so? But they simply come a-running. Repeat that again for me."

"As many times as you like. Listen, — a high-collared guy, swindler, bastard, super-swanker ..."

While I was repeating this, two shaky fellows came out of the room hammering the floor.

"Hey, you two gents, it won't do to run away. Won't let you off while I'm here. Come and have a drink. Bastard? That's fine. Bastardly fine. Now, come on."

And they pulled Porcupine and me away. These two fellows really had come to the lavatory, but soaked as they were, in booze bubbles, they apparently forgot to proceed to their original destination, and were pulling us hard. All booze fighters seem to be attracted by whatever comes directly under their eyes for the moment and forget what they had been proposing to do.

"Say, fellows, we've got bastards. Make them drink. Get them loaded. You gents got to stay here."

And they pushed me who never attempted to escape against the wall. Surveying the scene, I found there was no dish in which any edibles were left. Some one had eaten all his share, and gone on a foraging expedition. The principal was not there, — I did not know when he left.

At that time, preceded by a coquettish voice, three or four geishas entered the room. I was a bit surprised, but having been pushed against the wall, I had to look on quietly. At the instant, Red Shirt who had been leaning against a pillar with the same old amber pipe stuck into his mouth with some pride, suddenly got up and started to leave the room. One of the geishas who was advancing toward him smiled and courtesied at him as she passed by him. The geisha was the youngest and prettiest of the bunch. They were some distance away from me and I could not see very well, but it seemed that she might have said "Good evening." Red Shirt brushed past as if unconscious, and never showed again. Probably he followed the principal.

The sight of the geishas set the room immediately in a buzz and it became noisy as they all raised howls of welcome. Some started the game of "nanko" with a force that beat the sword-drawing practice. Others began playing morra, and the way they shook their hands, intently absorbed in the game, was a better spectacle than a puppet show.

One in the corner was calling "Hey, serve me here," but shaking the bottle, corrected it to "Hey, fetch me more sake." The whole room became so infernally noisy that I could scarcely stand it. Amid this orgy, one, like a fish out of water, sat down with his head bowed. It was Hubbard Squash. The reason they have held this farewell dinner party was not in order to bid him a farewell, but because they wanted to have a jolly good time for themselves with John Barleycorn. He had come to suffer only. Such a dinner party would have been better had it not been started at all.

After a while, they began singing ditties in outlandish voices. One of the geishas came in front of me, and taking up a samisen, asked me to sing something. I told her I didn't sing, but I'd like to hear, and she droned out:

"If one can go round and meet the one he wants, banging gongs and drums …… bang, bang, bang, bang, bing, shouting after wandering Santaro, there is some one I'd like to meet by banging round gongs and drums …… bang, bang, bang, bang, b-i-n-g."

She dashed this off in two breaths, and sighed, "O, dear!" She should have sung something easier.

Clown who had come near us meanwhile, remarked in his flippant tone:

"Hello, dear Miss Su-chan, too bad to see your beau go away so soon." The geisha pouted, "I don't know." Clown, regardless, began imitating "gidayu" with a dismal voice, — "What a luck, when she met her sweet heart by a rare chance..."

The geisha slapped the lap of Clown with a "Cut that out," and Clown gleefully laughed. This geisha is the one who made goo-goo eyes at Red Shirt. What a simpleton, to be pleased by the slap of a geisha, this Clown. He said:

"Say, Su-chan, strike up the string. I'm going to dance the Kiino-kuni." He seemed yet to dance.

On the other side of the room, the old man of Confucius, twisting round his toothless mouth, had finished as far as "...... dear Dembei-san" and is asking a geisha who sat in front of him to coach him for the rest. Old people seem to need polishing up their memorizing system. One geisha is talking to the teacher of natural history:

"Here's the latest. I'll sing it. Just listen. 'Margaret, the high-collared head with a white ribbon; she rides on a bike, plays a violin, and talks in broken English, — I am glad to see you.'" Natural history appears impressed, and says; "That's an interesting piece. English in it too."

Porcupine called "geisha, geisha," in a loud voice, and commanded; "Bang your samisen; I'm going to dance a sword-dance."

His manner was so rough that the geishas were

startled and did not answer. Porcupine, unconcerned, brought out a cane, and began performing the sword-dance in the center of the room. Then Clown, having danced the Kii-no-kuni, the Kap-pore and the Durhma-san on the Shelf, almost stark-naked, with a palm-fibre broom, began turkey-trotting about the room, shouting "The Sino-Japanese negotiations came to a break ...." The whole was a crazy sight.

I had been feeling sorry for Hubbard Squash, who up to this time had sat up straight in his full dress. Even were this a farewell dinner held in his honor, I thought he was under no obligation to look patiently in a formal dress at the naked dance. So I went to him and persuaded him with "Say, Koga-san, let's go home." Hubbard Squash said the dinner was in his honor, and it would be improper for him to leave the room before the guests. He seemed to be determined to remain.

"What do you care!" I said, "If this is a farewell dinner, make it like one. Look at those fellows; they're just like the inmates of a lunatic asylum. Let's go."

And having forced hesitating Hubbard Squash to his feet, we were just leaving the room, when Clown, marching past, brandishing the broom, saw us.

"This won't do for the guest of honor to leave before us," he hollered, "this is the Sino-Japanese negotiations. Can't let you off." He enforced his declaration by holding the broom across our way. My temper had been pretty well aroused for some time, and I felt impatient.

"The Sino-Japanese negotiation, eh? Then you're a Chink," and I whacked his head with a knotty fist.

This sudden blow left Clown staring blankly speechless for a second or two; then he stammered out:

"This is going some! Mighty pity to knock my head. What a blow on this Yoshikawa! This makes the Sino-Japanese negotiations the sure stuff."

While Clown was mumbling these incoherent remarks, Porcupine, believing some kind of row had been started, ceased his sword-dance and came running toward us. On seeing us, he grabbed the neck of Clown and pulled him back.

"The Sino-Japane ...... ouch! ...... ouch! This is outrageous," and Clown writhed under the grip of Porcupine who twisted him sideways and threw him down on the floor with a bang. I do not know the rest. I parted from Hubbard Squash on the way, and it was past eleven when I returned home.

CHAPTER X.

THE town is going to celebrate a Japanese victory to-day, and there is no school. The celebration is to be held at the parade ground, and Badger is to take out all the students and attend the ceremony. As one of the instructors, I am to go with them. The streets are everywhere draped with flapping national flags almost enough to dazzle the eyes. There were as many as eight hundred students in all, and it was arranged, under the direction of the teacher of physical culture to divide them into sections with one teacher or two to lead them. The arrangement itself was quite commendable, but in its actual operation the whole thing went wrong. All students are mere kiddies who, ever too fresh, regard it as beneath their dignity not to break all regulations. This rendered the provision of teachers among them practically useless. They would start marching songs without being told to, and if they ceased the marching songs, they would raise devilish shouts without cause. Their behavior would have done credit to the gang of tramps parading the streets demanding work. When they neither sing nor shout, they tee-hee and giggle. Why they cannot walk without these disorders, passes my understanding, but all Japanese are born with their mouths stuck out, and no kick will ever be strong enough to stop it. Their chatter is not only of simple nature, but about the teachers when their back is turned. What a degraded bunch! I made the students apologize to me on the dormitory affair, and considered the incident closed. But I was mistaken. To borrow the words of the old lady in the boarding house, I was surely wrong Mr. Wright. The apology they offered was not prompted by repentance in their hearts. They had kowtowed as a matter of form by the command of the principal. Like the tradespeople who bow their heads low but never give up cheating the public, the students apologize but never stop their mischiefs. Society is made up, I think it probable, of people just like those students. One may be branded foolishly honest if he takes seriously the apologies others might offer. We should regard all apologies a sham and forgiving also as a sham; then everything would be all right. If one wants to make another apologize from his heart, he has to pound him good and strong until he begs for mercy from his heart.

As I walked along between the sections, I could hear constantly the voices mentioning "tempura" or "dango." And as there were so many of them, I could not tell which one mentioned it. Even if I succeeded in collaring the guilty one I was sure of his saying, "No, I didn't mean you in saying tempura or dango. I fear you suffer from nervousness and make wrong inferences." This dastardly spirit has been fostered from the time of the feudal lords, and is deep-rooted. No amount of teaching or lecturing will cure it. If I stay in a town like this for one year or so, I may be compelled to follow their example, who knows, — clean and honest though I have been. I do not propose to make a fool of myself by remaining quiet when others attempt to play games on me, with all their excuses ready-made. They are men and so am I — students or kiddies or whatever they may be. They are bigger than I, and unless I get even with them by punishment, I would cut a sorry figure. But in the attempt to get even, if I resort to ordinary means, they are sure to make it a boomerang. If I tell them, "You're wrong," they will start an eloquent defence, because they are never short of the means of side-stepping. Having defended themselves, and made themselves appear suffering martyrs, they would begin attacking me. As the incident would have been started by my attempting to get even with them, my defence would not be a defence until I can prove their wrong. So the quarrel, which they had started, might be mistaken, after all, as one begun by me. But the more I keep silent the more they would become insolent, which, speaking seriously, could not be permitted for the sake of public morale. In consequence, I am obliged to adopt an identical policy so they cannot catch me in playing it back on them. If the situation comes to that, it would be the last day of the Yedo kid. Even so, if I am to be subjected to these pin-pricking tricks, I am a man and got to risk losing off the last remnant of the honor of the Yedo kid. I became more convinced of the advisability of returning to Tokyo quickly and living with Kiyo. To live long in such a country town would be like degrading myself for no purpose. Newspaper delivering would be preferable to being degraded so far as that.

I walked along with a sinking heart, thinking like this, when the head of our procession became suddenly noisy, and the whole came to a full stop. I thought something has happened, stepped to the right out of the ranks, and looked toward the direction of the noise. There on the corner of Otemachi, turning to Yakushimachi, I saw a mass packed full like canned sardines, alternately pushing back and forth. The teacher of physical culture came down the line hoarsely shouting to all to be quiet. I asked him what was the matter, and he said the middle school and the normal had come to a clash at the corner.

The middle school and the normal, I understood, are as much friendly as dogs and monkeys. It is not explained why but their temper was hopelessly crossed, and each would try to knock the chip off the shoulder of the other on all occasions. I presume they quarrel so much because life gets monotonous in this backwoods town. I am fond of fighting, and hearing of the clash, darted forward to make the most of the fun. Those foremost in the line are jeering, "Get out of the way, you country tax!"* while those in the rear are hollowing "Push them out!" I passed through the students, and was nearing the corner, when I heard a sharp command of "Forward!" and the line of the normal school began marching on. The clash which had resulted from contending for the right of way was settled, but it was settled by the middle school giving way to the normal. From the point of school-standing the normal is said to rank above the middle.

The ceremony was quite simple. The commander of the local brigade read a congratulatory address, and so did the governor, and the audience shouted banzais. That was all. The entertainments were scheduled for the afternoon, and I returned home at once and started writing to Kiyo an answer which

---

* The normal school in the province maintains the students mostly on the advance-expense system, supported by the country tax.

had been in my mind for some days. Her request had been that I should write her a letter with more detailed news; so I must get it done with care. But as I took up the rolled letter-paper, I did not know with what I should begin, though I have many things to write about.

Should I begin with that? That is too much trouble. Or with this? It is not interesting. Isn't there something which will come out smoothly, I reflected, without taxing my head too much, and which will interest Kiyo. There seemed, however, no such item as I wanted. I grated the ink-cake, wetted the writing brush, stared at the letter-paper — stared at the letter-paper, wetted the writing brush, grated the ink-cake — and, having repeated the same thing several times, I gave up the letter writing as not in my line, and covered the lid of the stationery box. To write a letter was a bother. It would be much simpler to go back to Tokyo and see Kiyo. Not that I am unconcerned about the anxiety of Kiyo, but to get up a letter to please the fancy of Kiyo is a harder job than to fast for three weeks.

I threw down the brush and letter-paper, and lying down with my bent arms as a pillow, gazed at the garden. But the thought of the letter to Kiyo would come back in my mind. Then I thought this way; If I am thinking of her from my heart, even at such a distance, my sincerity would find responsive appreciation in Kiyo. If it does find response, there is no need of sending letters. She will regard the absence of letters from me as a sign of my being in good health. If I write in case of illness or when something unusual happens, that will be sufficient.

The garden is about thirty feet square, with no particular plants worthy of name. There is one orange tree which is so tall as to be seen above the board fence from outside. Whenever I returned from the school I used to look at this orange tree. For to those who had not been outside of Tokyo, oranges on the tree are rather a novel sight. Those oranges now green will ripen by degrees and turn to yellow, when the tree would surely be beautiful. There are some already ripened. The old lady told me that they are juicy, sweet oranges. "They will all soon be ripe, and then help yourself to all you want," she said. I think I will enjoy a few every day. They will be just right in about three weeks. I do not think I will have to leave the town in so short a time as three weeks.

While my attention was centered on the oranges, Porcupine came in.

"Say, to-day being the celebration of victory, I thought I would get something good to eat with you, and bought some beef."

So saying, he took out a package covered with a bamboo-wrapper, and threw it down in the center of the room. I had been denied the pleasure of patronizing the noodle house or dango shop, on top of getting sick of the sweet potatoes and tofu, and I welcomed the suggestion with "That's fine," and began cooking it with a frying pan and some sugar borrowed from the old lady.

Porcupine, munching the beef to the full capacity of his mouth, asked me if I knew about Red Shirt having a favorite geisha. I asked if that was not one of the geishas who came to our dinner the other night, and he answered, "Yes, I got the wind of the fact only recently; you're sharp."

"Red Shirt always speaks of refinement of character or of mental consolation, but he is making a fool of himself by chasing round a geisha. What a dandy rogue. We might let that go if he wouldn't make fuss about others making fools of themselves. I understand through the principal he stopped your going even to noodle houses or dango shops as unbecoming to the dignity of the school, didn't he?"

"According to his idea, running after a geisha is a mental consolation but tempura or dango is a material pleasure, I guess. If that's mental consolation, why doesn't the fool do it above board? You ought to see the jackanapes skipping out of the room when the geisha came into it the other night, — I don't like his trying to deceive us, but if one were to point it out for him, he would deny it or say it was the Russian literature or that the haiku is a half-brother of the new poetry, and expect to hush it up by twaddling soft nonsense. A weak-knee like him is not a man. I believe he lived the life of a court-maid in former life. Perhaps his daddy might have been a kagema at Yushima in old days."

"What is a kagema?"

"I suppose something very unmanly, — sort of emasculated chaps. Say, that part isn't cooked enough. It might give you tape worm."

"So? I think it's all right. And, say, Red Shirt is said to frequent Kadoya at the springs town and meet his geisha there, but he keeps it in dark."

"Kadoya? That hotel?"

"Also a restaurant. So we've got to catch him

there with his geisha and make it hot for him right to his face."

"Catch him there? Suppose we begin a kind of night watch?"

"Yes, you know there is a rooming house called Masuya in front of Kadoya. We'll rent one room upstairs of the house, and keep peeping through a loophole we could make in the shoji."

"Will he come when we keep peeping at him?"

"He may. We will have to do it more than one night. Must expect to keep it up for at least two weeks."

"Say, that would make one pretty well tired, I tell you. I sat up every night for about one week attending my father when he died, and it left me thoroughly down and out for some time afterward."

"I don't care if I do get tired some. A crook like Red Shirt should not go unpunished that way for the honor of Japan, and I am going to administer a chastisement in behalf of heaven."

"Hooray! If things are decided upon that way, I am game. And we are going to start from to-night?"

"I haven't rented a room at Masuya yet, so can't start it to-night."

"Then when?"

"Will start before long. I'll let you know, and want you to help me."

"Right-O. I will help you any time. I am not much myself at scheming, but I am IT when it comes to fighting."

While Porcupine and I were discussing the plan of subjugating Red Shirt, the old lady appeared at the door, announcing that a student was wanting to see Professor Hotta. The student had gone to his house, but seeing him out, had come here as probable to find him. Porcupine went to the front door himself, and returning to the room after a while, said:

"Say, the boy came to invite us to go and see the entertainment of the celebration. He says there is a big bunch of dancers from Kochi to dance something, and it would be a long time before we could see the like of it again. Let's go."

Porcupine seemed enthusiastic over the prospect of seeing that dance, and induced me to go with him. I have seen many kinds of dance in Tokyo. At the annual festival of the Hachiman Shrine, moving stages come around the district, and I have seen the Shiokumi and almost any other variety. I was little inclined to see that dance by the sturdy fellows from Tosa province, but as Porcupine was so insistent, I changed my mind and followed him out. I did not know the student who came to invite Porcupine, but found he was the younger brother of Red Shirt. Of all students, what a strange choice for a messenger!

The celebration ground was decorated, like the wrestling amphitheater at Ryogoku during the season, or the annual festivity of the Hommonji temple, with long banners planted here and there, and on the ropes that crossed and recrossed in the mid-air were strung the colors of all nations, as if they were borrowed from as many nations for the occasion, and the large roof presented an unusually cheerful aspect. On the eastern corner there was built a temporary stage upon which the dance of Kochi was to be performed. For about half a block, with the stage on the right, there was a display of flowers and plant settings arranged on shelves sheltered with reed screens.

Everybody was looking at the display seemingly much impressed, but it failed to impress me. If twisted grasses or bamboos afforded so much pleasure, the gallantry of a hunchback or the husband of a wrong pair should give as much pleasure to their eyes.

In the opposite direction, aerial bombs and fire works were steadily going on. A balloon shot out on which was written "Long Live the Empire!" It floated leisurely over the pine trees near the castle tower, and fell down inside the compound of the barracks. Bang! A black ball shot up against the serene autumn sky; burst open straight above my head, streams of luminous green smoke ran down in an umbrella-shape, and finally faded. Then another balloon. It was red with "Long Live the Army and Navy" in white. The wind slowly carried it from the town toward the Aioi village. Probably it would fall into the yard of Kwanon temple there.

At the formal celebration this morning there were not quite so many as here now. It was a surging mass that made me wonder how so many people lived in the place. There were not many attractive faces among the crowd, but as far as the numerical strength went, it was a formidable one. In the meantime that dance had begun. I took it for granted that since they call it a dance, it would be something similar to the kind of dance by the Fujita troupe, but I was greatly mistaken.

Thirty fellows, dressed up in a martial style, in three rows of ten each, stood with glittering drawn swords. The sight was an eye-opener, indeed. The space between the rows measured about two feet, and that between the men might have been even less.

One stood apart from the group. He was similarly dressed but instead of a drawn sword, he carried a drum hung about his chest. This fellow drawled out signals the tone of which suggested a mighty easy-life, and then croaking a strange song, he would strike the drum. The tune was outlandishly unfamiliar. One might form an idea by thinking it a combination of the Mikawa Banzai and the Fudarakuya.

The song was drowsy, and like syrup in summer is dangling and slovenly. He struck the drum to make stops at certain intervals. The tune was kept with regular rhythmical order, though it appeared to have neither head nor tail. In response to this tune, the thirty drawn swords flash, with such dexterity and speed that the sight made the spectator almost shudder. With live men within two feet of their position, the sharp drawn blades, each flashing them in the same manner, they looked as if they might make a bloody mess unless they were perfectly accurate in their movements. If it had been brandishing swords alone without moving themselves, the chances of getting slashed or cut might have been less, but sometimes they would turn sideways together, or clear around, or bend their knees. Just one second's difference in the movement, either too quick or too late, on the part of the next fellow, might have meant sloughing off a nose or slicing off the head of the next fellow. The drawn swords moved in perfect freedom, but the sphere of action was limited to about two feet square, and to cap it all, each had to keep moving with those in front and back, at right and left, in the same direction at the same speed. This beats me! The dance of the Shiokumi or the Sekinoto would make no show compared with this! I heard them say the dance requires much training, and it could not be an easy matter to make so many dancers move in a unison like this. Particularly difficult part in the dance was that of the fellow with drum stuck to his chest. The movement of feet, action of hands, or bending of knees of those thirty fellows were entirely directed by the tune with which he kept them going. To the spectators this fellow's part appeared the easiest. He sang in a lazy tune, but it was strange that he was the fellow who takes the heaviest responsibility.

While Porcupine and I, deeply impressed, were looking at the dance with absorbing interest, a sudden hue and cry was raised about half a block off. A commotion was started among those who had been quietly enjoying the sights and all ran pell-mell in every direction. Some one was heard saying "fight!" Then the younger brother of Red Shirt came running forward through the crowd.

"Please, Sir," he panted, "a row again! The middles are going to get even with the normals and have just begun fighting. Come quick, Sir!" And he melted somewhere into the crowd.

"What troublesome brats! So they're at it again, eh? Why can't they stop it!"

Porcupine, as he spoke, dashed forward, dodging among the running crowd. He meant, I think, to stop the fight, because he could not be an idle spectator once he was informed of the fact. I of course had no intention of turning tail, and hastened on the heels of Porcupine. The fight was in its fiercest. There were about fifty to sixty normals, and the middles numbered by some ninety. The normals wore a uniform, but the middles had discarded their uniform and put on Japanese civilian clothes, which made the distinction between the two hostile camps easy. But they were so mixed up, and wrangling with such violence, that we did not know how and where we could separate them.

Porcupine, apparently at a loss what to do, looked at the wild scene awhile, then turned to me, saying:

"Let's jump in and separate them. It will be hell if cops get on them."

I did not answer, but rushed to the spot where the scuffle appeared most violent.

"Stop there! Cut this out! You're ruining the name of the school! Stop this, dash you!"

Shouting at the top of my voice, I attempted to penetrate the line which seemed to separate the hostile sides, but this attempt did not succeed. When about ten feet into the turmoil, I could neither advance nor retreat. Right in my front, a comparatively large normal was grappling with a middle about sixteen years of age.

"Stop that!"

I grabbed the shoulder of the normal and tried to force them apart when some one whacked my feet. On this sudden attack, I let go the normal and fell down sideways. Some one stepped on my back with heavy shoes. With both hands and knees upon the ground, I jumped up and the fellow on my back rolled off to my right. I got up, and saw the big body of Porcupine about twenty feet away, sandwiched between the students, being pushed back and forth, shouting, "Stop the fight! Stop that!"

"Say, we can't do anything!" I hollered at him, but unable to hear, I think, he did not answer.

A pebble-stone whiffled through the air and hit squarely on my cheek bone; the same moment some one banged my back with a heavy stick from behind.

"Profs mixing in!" "Knock them down!" was shouted.

"Two of them; big one and small. Throw stones at them!" Another shout.

"Drat you fresh jackanapes!" I cried as I wallopped the head of a normal nearby. Another stone grazed my head, and passed behind me. I did not know what had become of Porcupine, I could not find him. Well, I could not help it but jumped into the teapot to stop the tempest. I wasn't a Hottentot to skulk away on being shot at with pebble-stones. What did they think I was anyway! I've been through all kinds of fighting in Tokyo, and can take in all fights one may care to give me. I slugged, jabbed and banged the stuffing out of the fellow nearest to me. Then some one cried, "Cops! Cops! Cheese it! Beat it!" At that moment, as if wading through a pond of molasses, I could hardly move, but the next I felt suddenly released and both sides scampered off simultaneously. Even the country fellows do creditable work when it comes to retreating, more masterly than General Kuropatkin, I might say.

I searched for Porcupine who, I found, his overgown torn to shreds, was wiping his nose. He bled considerably, and his nose having swollen was a sight. My clothes were pretty well massed with dirt, but I had not suffered quite as much damage as Porcupine. I felt pain in my cheek and as Porcupine said, it bled some.

About sixteen police officers arrived at the scene but, all the students having beat it in opposite directions, all they were able to catch were Porcupine and me. We gave them our names and explained the whole story. The officers requested us to follow them to the police station which we did, and after stating to the chief of police what had happened, we returned home.

CHAPTER XI.

THE next morning on awakening I felt pains all over my body, due, I thought, to having had no fight for a long time. This is not creditable to my fame as regards fighting, so I thought while in bed, when the old lady brought me a copy of the Shikoku Shimbun. I felt so weak as to need some effort even reaching for the paper. But what man should be so easily upset by such a trifling affair, — so I forced myself to turn in bed, and, opening its second page, I was surprised. There was the whole story of the fight of yesterday in print. Not that I was surprised by the news of the fight having been published, but it said that one teacher Hotta of the Middle School and one certain saucy Somebody, recently from Tokyo, of the same institution, not only started this trouble by inciting the students, but were actually present at the scene of the trouble, directing the students and engaged themselves against the students of the Normal School. On top of this, something to the following effect was added.

"The Middle School in this prefecture has been an object of admiration by all other schools for its good and ideal behavior. But since this long-cherished honor has been sullied by these two irresponsible persons, and this city made to suffer the consequent indignity, we have to bring the perpetrators to full account. We trust that before we take any step in this matter, the authorities will have those 'toughs' properly punished, barring them forever from our educational circles."

All the types were italicized, as if they meant to administer typographical chastisement upon us. "What the devil do I care!" I shouted, and up I jumped out of bed. Strange to say, the pain in my joints became tolerable.

I rolled up the newspaper and threw it into the garden. Not satisfied, I took that paper to the cesspool and dumped it there. Newspapers tell such reckless lies. There is nothing so adept, I believe, as the newspaper in circulating lies. It has said what I should have said. And what does it mean by "one saucy Somebody who is recently from Tokyo?" Is there any one in this wide world with the name of Somebody? Don't forget, I have a family and personal name of my own which I am proud of. If they want to look at my family-record, they will bow before every one of my ancestors from Mitsunaka Tada down. Having washed my face, my cheek began suddenly smarting. I asked the old lady for a mirror, and she asked if I had read the paper of this morning. "Yes," I said, "and dumped it in the cesspool; go and pick it up if you want it," — and she withdrew with a startled look. Looking in the mirror, I saw bruises on my cheek. Mine is a precious face to me. I get my face bruised, and am called a saucy Somebody as if I were nobody. That is enough.

It will be a reflection on my honor to the end of my days if it is said that I shunned the public gaze and kept out of the school on account of the write-up in the paper. So, after breakfast, I attended the school ahead of all. One after the other, all coming to the school would grin at my face. What is there to laugh about! This face is my own, gotten up, I am sure, without the least obligation on their part. By and by, Clown appeared.

"Ha, heroic action yesterday. Wounds of honor, eh?"

He made this sarcastic remark, I suppose, in revenge for the knock he received on his head from me at the farewell dinner.

"Cut out nonsense; you get back there and suck your old drawing brushes!" Then he answered "that was going some," and enquired if it pained much?

"Pain or no pain, this is my face. That's none of your business," I snapped back in a furious temper. Then Clown took his seat on the other side, and still keeping his eye on me, whispered and laughed with the teacher of history next to him.

Then came Porcupine. His nose had swollen and was purple, — it was a tempting object for a surgeon's knife. His face showed far worse (is it my conceit that makes this comparison?) than mine. I and Porcupine are chums with desks next to each other, and moreover, as ill-luck would have it, the desks are placed right facing the door. Thus were two strange faces placed together. The other fellows, when in want of something to divert them, would gaze our way with regularity. They say "too bad," but they are surely laughing in their minds as "ha, these fools!" If that is not so, there is no reason for their whispering together and grinning like that. In the class room, the boys clapped their hands when I entered; two or three of them banzaied. I could not tell whether it was an enthusiastic approval or open insult. While I and Porcupine were thus being made the cynosures of the whole school, Red Shirt came to me as usual.

"Too bad, my friend; I am very sorry indeed for you gentlemen," he said in a semi-apologetic manner. "I've talked with the principal in regard to the story in the paper, and have arranged to demand that the paper retract the report, so you needn't worry on that score. You were plunged into the trouble because my brother invited Mr. Hotta, and I don't know how I can apologize to you! I'm going to do my level best in this matter; you gentlemen please depend on that." At the third hour recess the principal came out of his room, and seemed more or less perturbed, saying, "The paper made a bad mess of it, didn't it? I hope the matter will not become serious."

As to anxiety, I have none. If they propose to relieve me, I intend to tender my resignation before I get fired, — that's all. However, if I resign with no fault on my part, I would be simply giving the paper advantage. I thought it proper to make the paper take back what it had said, and stick to my position. I was going to the newspaper office to give them a piece of my mind on my way back but having been told that the school had already taken steps to have the story retracted, I did not.

Porcupine and I saw the principal and Red Shirt at a convenient hour, giving them a faithful version of the incident. The principal and Red Shirt agreed that the incident must have been as we said and that the paper bore some grudge against the school and purposely published such a story. Red Shirt made a round of personal visits on each teacher in the room, defending and explaining our action in the affair. Particularly he dwelt upon the fact that his brother invited Porcupine and it was his fault. All teachers denounced the paper as infamous and agreed that we two deserved sympathy.

On our way home, Porcupine warned me that Red Shirt smelt suspicious, and we would be done unless we looked out. I said he had been smelling some anyway, — it was not necessarily so just from to-day. Then he said that it was his trick to have us invited and mixed in the fight yesterday, — "Aren't you on to that yet?" Well, I was not. Porcupine was quite a Grobian but he was endowed, I was impressed, with a better brain than I.

"He made us mix into the trouble, and slipped behind and contrived to have the paper publish the story. What a devil!"

"Even the newspaper in the band wagon of Red Shirt? That surprises me. But would the paper listen to Red Shirt so easily?"

"Wouldn't it, though. Darn easy thing if one has friends in the paper."

"Has he any?"

"Suppose he hasn't, still that's easy. Just tell lies and say such and such are facts, and the paper will take it up."

"A startling revelation, this. If that was really a trick of Red Shirt, we're likely to be discharged on account of this affair."

"Quite likely we may be discharged."

"Then I'll tender my resignation tomorrow, and back to Tokyo I go. I am sick of staying in such a wretched hole."

"Your resignation wouldn't make Red Shirt squeal."

"That's so. How can he be made to squeal?"

"A wily guy like him always plots not to leave any trace behind, and it would be difficult to follow his track."

"What a bore! Then we have to stand in a false light, eh? Damn it! I call all kinds of god to witness if this is just and right!"

"Let's wait for two or three days and see how it turns out. And if we can't do anything else, we will have to catch him at the hot springs town."

"Leaving this fight affair a separate case?"

"Yes. We'll have to his hit weak spot with our own weapon."

"That may be good. I haven't much to say in planning it out; I leave it to you and will do anything at your bidding."

I parted from Porcupine then. If Red Shirt was really instrumental in bringing us two into the trouble as Porcupine supposed, he certainly deserves to be called down. Red Shirt outranks us in brainy work. And there is no other course open but to appeal to physical force. No wonder we never see the end of war in the world. Among individuals, it is, after all, the question of superiority of the fist.

Next day I impatiently glanced over the paper, the arrival of which I had been waiting with eagerness, but not a correction of the news or even a line of retraction could be found. I pressed the matter on Badger when I went to the school, and he said it might probably appear tomorrow. On that "tomorrow" a line of retraction was printed in tiny types. But the paper did not make any correction of the story. I called the attention of Badger to the fact, and he replied that that was about all that could be done under the circumstance. The principal, with the face like a badger and always swaggering, is surprisingly, wanting in influence. He has not even as much power as to bring down a country newspaper, which had printed a false story. I was so thoroughly indignant that I declared I would go alone to the office and see the editor-in-chief on the subject, but Badger said no.

"If you go there and have a blowup with the editor," he continued, "it would only mean your being handed out worse stuff in the paper again. Whatever is published in a paper, right or wrong, nothing can be done with it." And he wound up with a remark that sounded like a piece of sermon by a Buddhist bonze that "We must be contented by speedily despatching the matter from our minds and forgetting it."

If newspapers are of that character, it would be beneficial for us all to have them suspended, — the sooner the better. The similarity of the unpleasant sensation of being written-up in a paper and being bitten-down by a turtle became plain for the first time by the explanation of Badger.

About three days afterward, Porcupine came to me excited, and said that the time has now come, that he proposes to execute that thing we had planned out. Then I will do so, I said, and readily agreed to join him. But Porcupine jerked his head, saying that I had better not. I asked him why, and he asked if I had been requested by the principal to tender my resignation. No, I said, and asked if he had. He told me that he was called by the principal who was very, very sorry for him but under the circumstance requested him to decide to resign.

"That isn't fair. Badger probably had been pounding his belly-drum too much and his stomach is upside down," I said, "you and I went to the celebration, looked at the glittering sword dance together, and jumped into the fight together to stop it. Wasn't it so? If he wants you to tender your resignation, he should be impartial and should have asked me to also. What makes everything in the country school so dull-head. This is irritating!"

"That's wire-pulling by Red Shirt," he said. "I and Red Shirt cannot go along together, but they think you can be left as harmless."

"I wouldn't get along with that Red Shirt either. Consider me harmless, eh? They're getting too gay with me."

"You're so simple and straight that they think they can handle you in any old way."

"Worse still. I wouldn't get along with him, I tell you."

"Besides, since the departure of Koga, his successor has not arrived. Furthermore, if they fire me and you together, there will be blank spots in the schedule hours at the school."

"Then they expect me to play their game. Darn the fellow! See if they can make me."

On going to the school next day I made straightway for the room of the principal and started firing;

"Why don't you ask me to put in my resignation?" I said.

"Eh?" Badger stared blankly.

"You requested Hotta to resign, but not me. Is that right?"

"That is on account of the condition of the school ......"

"That condition is wrong, I dare say. If I don't have to resign, there should be no necessity for Hotta to resign either."

"I can't offer a detailed explanation about that ...... as to Hotta, it cannot be helped if he goes ...... we see no need of your resigning."

Indeed, he is a badger. He jabbers something, dodging the point, but appears complacent. So I had to say:

"Then, I will tender my resignation. You might have thought that I would remain peacefully while Mr. Hotta is forced to resign, but I cannot do it"

"That leaves us in a bad fix. If Hotta goes away and you follow him, we can't teach mathematics here."

"None of my business if you can't."

"Say, don't be so selfish. You ought to consider the condition of the school. Besides, if it is said that you resigned within one month of starting a new job, it would affect your record in the future. You should consider that point also."

"What do I care about my record. Obligation is more important than record."

"That's right. What you say is right, but be good enough to take our position into consideration. If you insist on resigning, then resign, but please stay until we get some one to take your place. At any rate, think the matter over once more, please."

The reason was so plain as to discourage any attempt to think it over, but as I took some pity on

Badger whose face reddened or paled alternately as he spoke, I withdrew on the condition that I would think the matter over. I did not talk with Red Shirt. If I have to land him one, it was better, I thought, to have it bunched together and make it hot and strong.

I acquainted Porcupine with the details of my meeting with Badger. He said he had expected it to be about so, and added that the matter of resignation can be left alone without causing me any embarrassment until the time comes. So I followed his advice. Porcupine appears somewhat smarter than I, and I have decided to accept whatever advices he may give.

Porcupine finally tendered his resignation, and having bidden farewell of all the fellow teachers, went down to Minato-ya on the beach. But he stealthily returned to the hot springs town, and having rented a front room upstairs of Masuya, started peeping through the hole he fingered out in the shoji. I am the only person who knows of this. If Red Shirt comes round, it would be night anyway, and as he is liable to be seen by students or some others during the early part in the evening, it would surely be after nine. For the first two nights, I was on the watch till about 11 o'clock, but no sign of Red Shirt was seen. On the third night, I kept peeping through from nine to ten thirty, but he did not come. Nothing made me feel more like a fool than returning to the boarding house at midnight after a fruitless watch. In four or five days, our old lady began worrying about me and advised me to quit night prowling, — being married. My night prowling is different from that kind of night prowling. Mine is that of administering a deserved chastisement. But then, when no encouragement is in sight after one week, it becomes tiresome. I am quick tempered, and get at it with all zeal when my interest is aroused, and would sit up all night to work it out, but I have never shone in endurance. However loyal a member of the heavenly-chastisement league I may be, I cannot escape monotony. On the sixth night I was a little tired, and on the seventh thought I would quit. Porcupine, however, stuck to it with bull-dog tenacity. From early in the evening up to past twelve, he would glue his eye to the shoji and keep steadily watching under the gas globe of Kadoya. He would surprise me, when I come into the room, with figures showing how many patrons there were to-day, how many stop-overs and how many women, etc. Red Shirt seems never to be coming, I said, and he would fold his arms, audibly sighing, "Well, he ought to." If Red Shirt would not come just for once, Porcupine would be deprived of the chance of handing out a deserved and just punishment.

I left my boarding house about 7 o'clock on the eighth night and after having enjoyed my bath, I bought eight raw eggs. This would counteract the attack of sweet potatoes by the old lady. I put the eggs into my right and left pockets, four in each, with the same old red towel hung over my shoulder, my hands inside my coat, went to Masuya. I opened the shoji of the room and Porcupine greeted me with his Idaten-like face suddenly radiant, saying:

"Say, there's hope! There's hope!" Up to last night, he had been downcast, and even I felt gloomy. But at his cheerful countenance, I too became cheerful, and before hearing anything, I cried, "Hooray! Hooray!"

"About half past seven this evening," he said, "that geisha named Kosuzu has gone into Kadoya."

"With Red Shirt?"

"No."

"That's no good then."

"There were two geishas ...... seems to me somewhat hopeful."

"How?"

"How? Why, the sly old fox is likely to send his girls ahead, and sneak round behind later."

"That may be the case. About nine now, isn't it?"

"About twelve minutes past nine," said he, pulling out a watch with a nickel case, "and, say put out the light. It would be funny to have two silhouettes of bonze heads on the shoji. The fox is too ready to suspect."

I blew out the lamp which stood upon the lacquer-enameled table. The shoji alone was dimly plain by the star light. The moon has not come up yet. I and Porcupine put our faces close to the shoji, watching almost breathless. A wall clock somewhere rang half past nine.

"Say, will he come to-night, do you think? If he doesn't show up, I quit."

"I'm going to keep this up while my money lasts."

"Money? How much have you?"

"I've paid five yen and sixty sen up to to-day for eight days. I pay my bill every night, so I can jump out anytime."

"That's well arranged. The people of this hotel must have been rather put out, I suppose."

"That's all right with the hotel; only I can't take my mind off the house."

"But you take some sleep in daytime."

"Yes, I take a nap, but it's nuisance because I can't go out."

"Heavenly chastisement is a hard job, I'm sure," I said. "If he gives us the slip after giving us such trouble, it would have been a thankless task."

"Well, I'm sure he will come to-night ... — ... Look, look!" His voice changed to whisper and I was alert in a moment. A fellow with a black hat looked up at the gas light of Kadoya and passed on into the darkness. No, it was not Red Shirt. Disappointing, this! Meanwhile the clock at the office below merrily tinkled off ten. It seems to be another bum watch to-night.

The streets everywhere had become quiet. The drum playing in the tenderloin reached our ears distinctively. The moon had risen from behind the hills of the hot springs. It is very light outside. Then voices were heard below. We could not poke our heads out of the window, so were unable to see the owners of the voices, but they were evidently coming nearer. The dragging of komageta (a kind of wooden footwear) was heard. They approached so near we could see their shadows.

"Everything is all right now. We've got rid of the stumbling block." It was undoubtedly the voice of Clown.

"He only glories in bullying but has no tact." This from Red Shirt.

"He is like that young tough, isn't he? Why, as to that young tough, he is a winsome, sporty Master Darling."

"I don't want my salary raised, he says, or I want to tender resignation, — I'm sure something is wrong with his nerves."

I was greatly inclined to open the window, jump out of the second story and make them see more stars than they cared to, but I restrained myself with some effort. The two laughed, and passed below the gas light, and into Kadoya.

"Say."

"Well."

"He's here."

"Yes, he has come at last."

"I feel quite easy now."

"Damned Clown called me a sporty Master Darling."

"The stumbling block means me. Hell!"

I and Porcupine had to waylay them on their return. But we knew no more than the man in the moon when they would come out. Porcupine went down to the hotel office, notifying them to the probability of our going out at midnight, and requesting them to leave the door unfastened so we could get out anytime. As I think about it now, it is wonderful how the hotel people complied with our request. In most cases, we would have been taken for burglars.

It was trying to wait for the coming of Red Shirt, but it was still more trying to wait for his coming out again. We could not go to sleep, nor could we remain with our faces stuck to the shoji all the time with our minds constantly in a state of feverish agitation. In all my life, I never passed such fretful, mortifying hours. I suggested that we had better go right into his room and catch him but Porcupine rejected the proposal outright. If we get in there at this time of night, we are likely to be prevented from preceding much further, he said, and if we ask to see him, they will either answer that he is not there or will take us into a different room. Supposing we do break into a room, we cannot tell of all those many rooms, where we can find him. There is no other way but to wait for him to come out, however tiresome it may be. So we sat up till five in the morning.

The moment we saw them emerging from Kadoya, I and Porcupine followed them. It was some time before the first train started and they had to walk up to town. Beyond the limit of the hot springs town, there is a road for about one block running through the rice fields, both sides of which are lined with cedar trees. Farther on are thatch-roofed farm houses here and there, and then one comes upon a dyke leading straight to the town through the fields. We can catch them anywhere outside the town, but thinking it would be better to get them, if possible, on the road lined with cedar trees where we may not be seen by others, we followed them cautiously. Once out of the town limit, we darted on a double-quick time, and caught up with them. Wondering what was coming after them, they turned back, and we grabbed their shoulders. We cried, "Wait!" Clown, greatly rattled, attempted to escape, but I stepped in front of him to cut off his retreat.

"What makes one holding the job of a head teacher stay over night at Kadoya!" Porcupine directly fired the opening gun.

"Is there any rule that a head teacher should not stay over night at Kadoya?" Red Shirt met the attack in a polite manner. He looked a little pale.

"Why the one who is so strict as to forbid others from going even to noodle houses or dango shops as unbecoming to instructors, stayed over night at a hotel with a geisha!"

Clown was inclined to run at the first opportunity; so kept I before him.

"What's that Master Darling of a young tough!" I roared.

"I didn't mean you. Sir. No, Sir, I didn't mean you, sure." He insisted on this brazen excuse. I happened to notice at that moment that I had held my pockets with both hands. The eggs in both pockets jerked so when I ran, that I had been holding them, I thrust my hand into the pocket, took out two and dashed them on the face of Clown. The eggs crushed, and from the tip of his nose the yellow streamed down. Clown was taken completely surprised, and uttering a hideous cry, he fell down on the ground and begged for mercy. I had bought those eggs to eat, but had not carried them for the purpose of making "Irish Confetti" of them. Thoroughly roused, in the moment of passion, I had dashed them at him before I knew what I was doing. But seeing Clown down and finding my hand grenade successful, I banged the rest of the eggs on him, intermingled with "Darn you, you sonovagun!" The face of Clown was soaked in yellow.

While I was bombarding Clown with the eggs, Porcupine was firing at Red Shirt.

"Is there any evidence that I stayed there over night with a geisha?"

"I saw your favorite old chicken go there early in the evening, and am telling you so. You can't fool me!"

"No need for us of fooling anybody. I stayed there with Mr. Yoshikawa, and whether any geisha had gone there early in the evening or not, that's none of my business."

"Shut up!" Porcupine walloped him one. Red Shirt tottered.

"This is outrageous! It is rough to resort to force before deciding the right or wrong of it!"

"Outrageous indeed!" Another clout. "Nothing but walloping will be effective on you scheming guys." The remark was followed by a shower of blows. I soaked Clown at the same time, and made him think he saw the way to the Kingdom-Come. Finally the two crawled and crouched at the foot of a cedar tree, and either from inability to move or to see, because their eyes had become hazy, they did not even attempt to break away.

"Want more? If so, here goes some more!" With that we gave him more until he cried enough. "Want more? You?" we turned to Clown, and he answered "Enough, of course."

"This is the punishment of heaven on you grovelling wretches. Keep this in your head and be more careful hereafter. You can never talk down justice."

The two said nothing. They were so thoroughly cowed that they could not speak.

"I'm going to neither run away nor hide. You'll find me at Minato-ya on the beach up to five this evening. Bring police officers or any old thing you want," said Porcupine.

"I'm not going to run away or hide either. Will wait for you at the same place with Hotta. Take the case to the police station if you like, or do as you damn please," I said, and we two walked our own way.

It was a little before seven when I returned to my room. I started packing as soon as I was in the room, and the astonished old lady asked me what I was trying to do. I'm going to Tokyo to fetch my Madam, I said, and paid my bill. I boarded a train and came to Minato-ya on the beach and found Porcupine asleep upstairs. I thought of writing my resignation, but not knowing how, just scribbled off that "because of personal affairs, I have to resign and return to Tokyo. Yours truly," and addressed and mailed it to the principal.

The steamer leaves the harbor at six in the evening. Porcupine and I, tired out, slept like logs, and when we awoke it was two o'clock. We asked the maid if the police had called on us, and she said no. Red Shirt and Clown had not taken it to the police, eh? We laughed.

That night I and Porcupine left the town. The farther the vessel steamed away from the shore, the more refreshed we felt. From Kobe to Tokyo we boarded a through train and when we made Shimbashi, we breathed as if we were once more in congenial human society. I parted from Porcupine at the station, and have not had the chance of meeting him since.

I forgot to tell you about Kiyo. On my arrival at Tokyo, I rushed into her house swinging my valise, before going to a hotel, with "Hello, Kiyo, I'm back!"

"How good of you to return so soon!" she cried and hot tears streamed down her cheeks. I was overjoyed, and declared that I would not go to the country any more but would start housekeeping with Kiyo in Tokyo.

Some time afterward, some one helped me to a job as assistant engineer at the tram car office. The salary was 25 yen a month, and the house rent six. Although the house had not a magnificent front entrance, Kiyo seemed quite satisfied, but, I am sorry to say, she was a victim of pneumonia and died in February this year. On the day preceding her death, she asked me to her bedside, and said, "Please, Master Darling, if Kiyo is dead, bury me in the temple yard of Master Darling. I will be glad to wait in the grave for my Master Darling."

So Kiyo's grave is in the Yogen temple at Kobinata.

— **(THE END)** —

Abstract

This English translation of 坊っちゃん (1906) was published in Tokyo by Ogawa Seibundo in 1918. It is a first-person narrative of a young man's two-month tenure as assistant mathematics teacher at a provincial middle school in 1890s Japan. A native son of Tokyo, with all its traits and prejudices, he finds life in a narrow country town unappealing — with its dull and mischievous students, scheming faculty, bland diets, stifling rules, and gossipy inhabitants. Impulsive, combative, committed to strict ideals of honesty, honor, and justice, he is quickly enmeshed in the strategems of the head teacher, "Red Shirt." His sufferings and confusion continue to mount until finally he and fellow-teacher "Porcupine" are able to deliver a "heavenly chastisement" and escape the island, back to his one emotional attachment, Kiyo, the old family retainer.

Natsume Kinnosuke (1867-1916) signed his work Sōseke — "stubborn." Like the narrator of *Botchan,* he was a city-born Tokyo-ite, who found himself teaching middle school in remote Matsuyama in Shikoku in 1895. He emerged to study English literature in London, become Professor at Tokyo Imperial University, and a successful novelist, beginning with the popular *I Am a Cat* in 1905.

Natsume Kinnosuke in 1891, age 24.

Notes

58.7   Mitsunaka Tada] (912–987 A.D) a famous Shōgun during the Heian Period.

66.28   Maruki a photographer of Shibaku] Maruki Riyō (丸木 利陽, 1854–1923) was a prominent Japanese photographer during the late-Meiji period.

112.27   the old wooden bucket and the morning glory.] 朝顔に　釣瓶とられて　貰い水 ： Morning glories / Entwined in the bucket at the well / So, I beg for water. — Chiyo-ni (1703–1775), a student under two of Basho's apprentices.

136.2-3   to celebrate a Japanese victory] In the First Sino-Japanese War, hostilities began in July 1894 and continued through March 1895. The Japanese army and navy scored a series of victories at sea and in Korea and Manchuria.

149.25   General Kuropatkin,] Aleksey Kuropatkin (1848–1925) was Russian army commander during the Russo-Japanese War of 1904-1905. His mismanagement contributed to the Russian defeat.

155.10   Grobian] A coarse, uncouth, uncivilized man; from German, *Grobian* — boor, lout.